ABSOLUTE LOVE

JA'NESE DIXON

PUBLISHING

ISBN-13: 978-1-950405-08-4 (paperback)

Printed in the United States of America.

CONTENTS

SNEAK PEEK: ROCKSTAR SECRETS

Can two people so different find love?

I'm sitting in a luncheon and my boss announces that I'm the first female African American partner under the age of thirty in the history of the firm.

I'm Ryann Gibson. I practice corporate law by day and hang with my guys by night, as a partner of Platinum Prestige. My bank account is fat, my house is laid, but my bed is cold and empty.

Dating at this stage of my life mirrors the setup of a bad joke. What do you get when you...fill in the blank? Meet an old guy? Meet a broke guy? Meet a young guy?

When Xavier, our waiter, asks me out I wait for the rest of the joke. Because he has three strikes against him.

He's young, cocky, and he just quit his job. His confidence intrigues me and our instant attraction has me saying yes when I should say no.

1

Little do I know, I'm signing up for the ride of my life. Nor how this one concession sets my cold bed ablaze and all work, no play becomes all night, all day.

But when the smoke clears, can two people so different find love?

a trail of sweat trickles down my spine. I lean forward with my gaze focused on the podium across the room. The intimate venue sits inside Torsion, one of Austin's premier restaurants. My firm, Colin, Baker & Garrett, hosts its annual luncheon on Labor Day to announce the new partners.

"Breathe ma." I turn my nose towards the smile of his cologne. The waiter smiles, darting his eyes towards Ryker Colin, the managing partner. "Your face gave you away."

I'm a wreck. This is the third year I've sat through this luncheon sure Ryker would call my name. Today's no different.

The silver pitcher crosses my path, and I glance back up at the waiter. His brown eyes resemble the way I take my coffee, black with a splash of milk. I didn't notice him before, but I do now.

I nod to send him on his way because at this point I'm just listening for my name. He refills my glass with more water then he turns to leave. His shoulders are broad and fill out his crisp white shirt to perfection. He glances back, his eyes linger over my face then dip lower.

Look at him.

Most men, including present company, don't see me as a woman. I'm the competition, even though we work for the same firm. I respect his confidence.

"Thank you, Xavier." The silver name tag sits on his massive chest.

"You're welcome."

I watch him pass through the sea of tables until he stops at the back of the room. He points from one end to the other as the waiters disperse around the room.

"Enjoy your meals." Ryker nods his head, retaking his seat near the front of the room.

"What did I miss?"

"Nothing. I should be asking you the same." Scott tips his head towards Xavier.

"Stop."

"What?" He laughs, but I have to cancel whatever is dancing around in his very active head. Scott's the office playboy, so he believes every man is sniffing around waiting for their next conquest. But I'm not that type of chick, at all.

"Eat." I point at the plate lowered in front of him grabbing my glass. I take a drink, wanting to run it across my forehead and neck. But I refuse to ruin my makeup or let them see me sweat.

"Ryann Gibson, you're no fun," he dips closer, "when you need to get laid."

I gasp at his retort, and the water slips down the wrong pipe. I'm choking. Scott has laughter in his eyes as he reaches to pat my back, but he's beat by another steady hand. I glance up, and it's Xavier. His touch sends shock waves through my body.

"You good?" His smile is kind and causes little wrinkles to gather in the corners of his eyes.

"Uh-huh. Thanks again." I slump forward to avoid his touch.

"No problem." He's off again, and this time I'm not the only one watching his departure.

Scott leans over my shoulder. "I know you won't ask for my opinion. But as your friend, co-counsel, drinking buddy, and I'd say I'm your best friend if you didn't have the guys vying for the position…"

I laugh using the napkin to dry my eyes. *Damn water.*

"I think you have an admirer."

"I'm ignoring you and eating this unseasoned chicken while I wait for these people to come to their senses." I glance at Scott, who has the deepest blue eyes I've ever seen.

"Think about it. A quickie with a waiter." Scott's sarcasm is dry and boring. Let him tell it, he's the only one for me.

My head snaps in his direction. *I can't deal with this*

man. I don't have time for men or the craziness that comes with them. I politely ignore Scott and pick up my fork. I inspect the chicken breast, steamed potatoes, and green beans. Expensive food doesn't always mean it's good food. I shrug. I have time to kill since they save the announcement until the end of the luncheon.

Scott grabs his fork, starting up a conversation with the associate beside him. He and I started as interns together. We joined the firm the same year, yet they promoted him to partner two years ago.

We've spent many nights marveling over the fact that they've passed me up twice. I was pissed, but I'm proud of my friend. He's happily rubbing elbows with the big dogs at the firm while I'm still proving myself. I take a deep breath hoping and praying my early days, late nights, and Saturdays prove to the firm that I'm partner material. I can't imagine where I'd be if it weren't for my best friends and business partners at Platinum Prestige. Probably curled up in a puddle of tears.

My mind races with ultimatums, should they not promote me again. Because in reality, I don't need this job. Platinum Prestige is booming, and as an equal partner, I can walk away from practicing law at any time. That and the trust fund from my grandparents.

It's been about five years since the ten of us—Hunter, Harper, Charlee, Parker, Taylor, Chase, Jordan, Payton, Alex, and I—turned the idea of an elite concierge service into a multi-million dollar company. Our clientele grows daily, and it's even brought in many clients into my corporate law practice. I've worked my ass off for this firm.

It's now or never.

"Excuse me, Miss Gibson." I look up to see a young woman with stars in her eyes. I remember those days.

"Please call me Ryann." I pat the empty seat beside me.

"My name is Dominique. I'm clerking with the firm this summer."

"Congratulations. How's it going?"

"Well, I think."

We laugh. "I know the feeling. Are you a second-year student?"

"Yes, ma'am I'm at the University of Texas. You're the reason I applied here."

"Really?"

She nods. "You spoke at a career day my junior year in high school. So, I wanted to thank you personally." Her eyes glisten with unshed tears.

"Don't you dare." I tease, passing her a napkin. "You had to do the work to get here. But I'm glad to have contributed in any way I could to get you here."

"You made me believe I could do it."

"And I was right." I hug her and pass her my card. "Let's get together for coffee or lunch."

"Yes, ma'am." She holds the card to her chest like its a prized possession. "Enjoy the rest of the luncheon."

"You too." She walks away. We need more talented woman of color around this firm.

My emotions swirl and I drop my head, getting my

feelings in check. I stand to excuse myself. These stuffy men in suits do not determine my value. I know it, and I remind myself with each exhale. Young women like Dominique are why I stay.

I visit the ladies room and step out to find Xavier leaning against the wall. A pleased look covers his face. I'm not attracted to beards, but his might change my mind.

"Xavier, are you waiting for someone?" I scan the hallway.

He stands from the wall, taking a few steps in my direction. "I didn't get your name."

I glance up, extending a hand. "Ryann."

I estimate he's a few inches taller than me. I'm sure his size intimidates most, but I'm six feet myself.

"Ryann, I was waiting for you." He smiles with a chuckle brushing his thumb across the tip of his nose. He breaks eye contact for a second before turning back.

"Yo X, congrats man." Another waiter passes by, and Xavier taps fists with him.

"Thanks, man. I'll see you on Friday?"

"No doubt."

We're alone again, and Xavier turns back to me. "I'd like to take you out."

"Congrats? Did you get a promotion?"

"Not exactly. It's my last day."

"Oh, really." I step aside to let someone pass. "What's next for you?"

"I got plans. I'll tell you all about it over dinner."

"Are you old enough to date?" I tease to bring my hormones under control because my senses are on an epic roller coaster, from nervous to agitated to flattered. "No shade." I hold back a laugh.

"That sounds shady as hell." His mouth twists as if in deep thought with his eyes peering through his thick eyelashes down into mine. "I got you ma. Kick it with me, Friday night."

"*Kick it*...with you?" I point at him, pronouncing every letter and syllable sounding boujee as hell.

Xavier is handsome, I'll give him that, but he looks no more than twenty-three, twenty-four, tops. And I'm adding a few of those years purely on the strength of his full facial hair. It gives him a mature appearance.

"Yes, Ryann, with me."

He leans back with open hands before dropping them in front of his bulky body. One hand clasping the wrist of the other, giving off an aura that I've seen a few men possess, namely Denzel Washington, Barak Obama, Shawn Carter. Those kinds of men. That *I'm the man*— even on my worse day—type of look.

I get a good look. I start from his close crop hair swimming in waves, not excessive, but it shows he takes pride in his appearance. I take my time ending at his polished dress shoes. His swag is on one thousand.

"My father always says, 'You study long. You study wrong.'" He adds with a cocky grin.

The energy passing between us is explosive, and I'm

not beneath enjoying a beautiful specimen such as Xavier but…

"It's one date, not forever…yet." He licks his lips, and I glance over my shoulder at the luncheon to bring my temperature down a few notches. "Friday night, I'll pick you up, you'll be my special guest."

"Special guest?" I turn back, and he's closer. I stand straighter next to him. Even in my heels, I have to look up to meet his intense gaze.

"That's right. I'd love nothing more than to play this little game with you ma, but I have an appointment. All I need is your address." He passes his phone, and I stare at it.

"I didn't say yes." I cross my hands over my chest, bringing us closer.

"You won't have to pull out your wallet. I'm not a wack-ass chump that doesn't know how to treat a beautiful woman, such as yourself. I'll get you to and from your home safely. So what do you say gorgeous?"

"Beautiful, gorgeous, laying it on pretty thick?"

"I'm gunning for date number two." The cocky smirk and intensity in his eyes are sending smoke signals warning my heart, *Don't let the smooth baby skin and smooth tenor voice fool you.*

I'm beyond youthful mistakes. My days of letting a panty dropper bag me are long gone. It's not to say I don't know how to satisfy my womanly needs, when needed, but a third leg and fat wallet doesn't rule me. Because I have my own coins and batteries are $5.99.

"Just know I'll be packing." I strum my fingers over the edge of my purse.

"You won't need your heat with me baby, but if it makes you feel secure." He shrugs, seemingly unfazed by my attempts to sidestep this date. "Your address."

I hesitate. He already knows where I work, meeting him at my home wouldn't be smart, especially if he's looking for a sugar mamma.

"Let's meet at Smith & Jameson in the warehouse district."

"That's fine. I'll pick you up at nine o'clock." His phone is still hanging between us. "Damn, I've never had to plead a *case* to get a chick's number. But it's all good."

I roll my eyes and take it. "What should I wear?"

"Whatever makes you happy. It's a gathering for my company." He drops his phone in his pocket.

"Your company?"

He nods while typing on his screen. "Urban sexy chic is how my sister describes it. Just no jeans." My phone chimes. " I need to run. I'll see you in a few days."

He extends a hand, and I accept. Much like his height, his large hand engulfs mine.

"I'm curious. How tall are you?"

"Six three." He lifts my hand to his mouth, his lips softly brush against the back, and I can barely swallow. My body's working overtime from a little kiss. "Congratulations on your promotion."

"I didn't get it yet."

"You will."

Oh, this man is good. "Thank you."

"You're welcome. Tell me all about it on Friday because I need to run."

Xavier pulls away, and I step back watching him leave. I glance at my hand, and it still tingles from his touch. I fall back against the wall until the sound of Ryker's voice fills the hallway. I yank upright to get back inside.

It's time.

CHAPTER 2

I'm free. I step outside Torsion loosening my tie. Seven years of my life ended today. No more filling in for "sick" employees, no more late nights and early mornings, no more getting paid less than I'm worth.

I saved every penny, worked overtime, reinvested in my artists and my company. My heart grips. *Shit, I'm getting emotional.*

I tip my head back. The sky appears bluer, the skyscrapers are higher and more reflective as the sun bounces between the buildings. The rooftop pool in the distance kicks me into gear.

My father's right, "Humble beginnings make the best stories." I'm writing this story and riding it until the wheels fall off. Hell, I'll still turn a few corners on the rims to keep moving forward.

I laugh, pulling out my phone to call my dad.

"It's official. I'm on my way."

"You're the man now. How does it feel?"

"Man, Pops, it feels unreal I'm officially the CEO of Brand X Entertainment exclusively." I struggle to put one foot in front of the other. But I have a staff meeting.

"Congratulations, you deserve it. How's your day looking? We can grab a celebratory drink later."

"I'll make time for that. I'll hit you back later. Love you."

"Love you too. Don't forget to call your Mom and tell her the good news yourself."

"Yes, sir. I'm off, Dad. Tia is waiting for me with major attitude." I see her near the curb, tapping the face of her watch.

"Lord help that child if she has to wait more than five seconds. Bossy since the day she was born." I chuckle as his boisterous laugh carries through the line. But he's right. "Drinks on me later. Call me, and I'll be there."

"Yes, sir." I disconnect the call taking a step, I glance back once more, hoping to catch a glimpse of Ryann. I didn't expect to get a yes from her. That woman is six foot something of all body. But her smile changed everything. It feels cliche as fuck, but it took my breath away, slow and deadly.

Ain't that some shit.

I spotted her the moment I entered the hall. I scheduled myself for a few hours to complete my outgoing paperwork then found myself working the luncheon. But thanks to an employee calling in, I met Ryann.

I stop outside my Range Rover. Tia leans against the door waiting for me to climb inside. I drop my head back and smile over at her.

"What took you so long? I thought you changed your mind."

"About quitting? No, it is done, and I'm all in."

"It's about time. You should've done it years ago." She pulls away from the curb. "Thanks for letting me borrow your ride. My car is still in the shop. They have to replace the entire windshield." She shakes her head in disgust.

"That'll set you back a couple of grand."

"Tell me about it."

We hit the highway heading to the old East Austin, now Central Austin thanks to gentrification. A few years ago, we bought a block of abandoned buildings. Now, we're worth millions in real estate alone.

She pulls up behind the office building, cutting the engine. "I'm proud of you Baby Bro."

"Why?" I rub at my tired eyes still overwhelmed by it all. I've planned and planned, and now here I am.

"Fishing for compliments?" She wraps her arms around the stirring wheel.

"Stop stalling." I pull on her waist-length braids.

My big sister's held down Brand X Entertainment while I maintained my full-time managerial position at Torsion. We had a payroll to maintain. Working as a manager kept the cashflow fluid. So, I didn't want to cut the cord too soon. But I promised to turn in my letter of resignation once we signed our fifth act, and we did last month.

An acoustic-soul singer named Cash. He's part hippie, Jon B, and Justin Timberlake. It's a hell of a mix. And before the ink dried on his contract, things went bananas starting a bidding war.

"I guess…" She glances over at me, and I feel her emotions. She's my twin, my identical twin. I'd do anything for her, and she'd do the same to me. "I appreciate you, is all."

"No tears allowed." I sit up and pull her close, and I kiss her forehead. She's had a rough couple of years.

"Come on because I have to pick up Tyson." She pushes a braid behind her ear.

"Go grab him and bring him back."

"You sure?" She stops glancing down at her watch.

"Yeah, they can wait. Plus, I'll change and get my notes together."

She climbs back inside. "Don't start without me."

"I won't." I walk up to the building as she pulls out of the parking lot. "Don't forget to feed my nephew."

"Bye, X! I'll be back."

I laugh to the front doors. I open the glass doors nodding my greeting to the receptionist and the security guard. We're all about business, but family comes first.

An aerial view of the block would show the building in a "X" shape. This building sits in the intersection. It's the heart of Brand X Entertainment. The first floor holds offices, the mailroom, two conference rooms, security, and the receptionist bay. The second floor contains the executive offices, a large conference room, Tyson's playroom, and my studio apartment.

I stop by my office to check my emails. Then I send a quick message to the staff about the meeting time change. I await all the appropriate responses before heading to my apartment.

I unlock the door and step inside. I turn on the light closing the door behind me. Tia, my parents, and I share this floor, but sometimes the staff uses the conference room on this floor because it's larger and has a fantastic view of Austin.

I shower and change into my street gear. Then drop to the couch. Today is a milestone. I look at my wall of remembrance and head over. I grab an index card from the side table and scribble the date and line item...*Resigned from Torsion.* I add it to the others.

People thought I was crazy for keeping that job for seven years, especially after we hit a million in revenue. But my entire family, my folks and my sister, are on my payroll. One mishap, or bad business deal, and it wouldn't just affect me but them too. I can't have that on my conscious, not after asking them to join me on this adventure.

My mother handles the finances. My father manages the personnel. My sister is my right-hand woman and handles the day-to-day business operations. I'm all about the talent, artist management, and establishing our brand presence.

"Who is it?" I smile, turning to the door. The signature knock rings through the room. Then a little extra lingers on the end.

"Me!" He yells with a squeak in his voice.

"Me who?"

"Me, Uncle X. Tyson."

I open the door, and he dives towards me. I rough him up then pull him into my arms. He holds on tight to his Happy Meal with one arm around my neck.

"Mmmmm…. smells like nuggets. Good cause I'm hungry."

"I got barbecue sauce too." His face looks exactly like mine. I sit on the couch, and he wiggles until he's comfortable on my leg. He opens the box and examines each item. "A toy. Some fries." He pops one in my mouth. "Some nuggets."

"How many nuggets do you have?"

He passes me the box, and I sit it on the couch beside us. He opens it, careful not to drop any. Then he starts counting. "Ten."

"That sounds like a big kid's meal to me."

"That's because it is." Tia walks in and sits across from us. "That boy is turning into the human eating machine."

"Like Uncle X?" His beaming toothless grin is contagious.

"Yes, just like your Uncle X. Now hurry and eat. Grams is coming to pick you up."

I kiss the top of his head, and he lowers to the floor, placing his box and drink on the coffee table. I spend a lot of time between these walls, especially with balancing several hats. CEO, manager, producer, son, brother, uncle. It's my spot in the city since my house is in the country.

Tyson opens the container wide pulling out the nuggets with two hands. He opens the carton wide, then reaches back for his fries. I glance over at Tia. Hair did, nails did. She's a fighter and an exceptional mother, raising an extraordinary son.

I'm always baffled at how she manages him and us without breaking her stride. Tia leans forward to help him, I stop her with a hand. Our connection means no words are needed. She nods, sitting back in the seat.

Tyson meticulously lays out his meal before kneeling in front of the table to eat. And when he's pleased with the arrangement his hands clap together. "Amen."

"Amen." We say in agreement.

"You need a minute to get ready?" I ask Tia, pulling her gaze from Tyson, our little man is growing up.

"Yeah, I need to grab my notes and review a few numbers for the listening party Friday."

"Go get ready. I got him."

She nods, standing to leave. *That's your child,* she mouths before heading out to her office.

I laugh. I guess it's the same DNA thing because he's exactly like me. Tyson dips a nugget and passes it to me. I take a bite and make a show of rubbing my belly.

He giggles, dancing a little then he turns back to his meal.

"How was school?" I sit on the floor beside him.

"Good."

"Are you hanging with me this weekend?" Tia's taking college classes on the weekends. I alternate babysitting with our folks.

He shakes his head while drinking from the tiny cup. "Mommy said no, my daddy is coming."

Heat laced with anger lines my heart, and I drop my chin to hide my face. I glance at my hands in my lap, combing my mind. I don't recall Tia mentioning. I take a deep breath because I can't let him hear the hate I have for his father in my voice. "He is. When?"

Tyson stops bouncing the nugget in the sauce, it's like my eyes looking back at me. "In one, two, three, four, five, six sleeps." He drops the nugget counting across his fingers. I force a smile. "Are you mad because of me, Uncle X?"

"Never." I gather him to me. "Never ever would I be mad at you. You're my Little Man. Right?"

He nods. This "at me" stuff started a few months ago. Are you sad because of me? Are you mad because of me? Are you crying because of me?

His father bouncing in and out of his life makes him believe it's all his fault. I could kill the man. And I'd gladly plead guilty and serve my time. Because no kid should feel the burden of his parent's failures.

"Look at who I found." Tia enters the room.

Tyson grabs my cheeks and kisses the top of my head. I guess he got that from me too. Our eyes hold, "Remember what I told you?"

"You love me more than life." Tyson recites.

"Don't forget it." I squeeze him tight. This means it will be a long weekend.

"Yes, sir." His face scrunches up, and I brace myself. "How much is that Uncle X?"

I chuckle, and my love for him overwhelms me. I can't imagine what having my own children will feel like because this guy has my whole heart.

"Now imagine this." I reach for his last chicken nugget, holding it up. "Think about how many of these it would take to fill this entire building." His eyes buck wide scanning the room as if his little imagination is about to explode. "I love you more than that Tyson."

His arms wrap around my neck. "That's a lot of chicken Uncle X."

"It is." I stand up laughing and place Tyson on his feet. "Grab your stuff. Oh, and there's a bag in that drawer."

His eyebrows shoot up. He runs across the room to "the drawer" where I keep gifts stashed for him. He yanks it open and jumps up and down.

Tia rounds the couch trying to read my thoughts, as my mother stands behind her. I hope the creep comes like he promised, but just in case I'll have to love extra hard on my Little Man.

"Open it when you get to Grams. Then call me. Okay?"

"Yeeeessss sir." He's bouncing back and forth, side to side.

"X." Tia places a hand on her hip.

"That's what uncles are for. Right, Little Man?"

"Yeah!" His little fist pumps in the air.

"Bring it in so you can leave. We have work to do. I gotta be able to afford all those Happy Meals."

He sprints across the room, and I catch him. I hold him close. "Behave for Grams and Pop Pop."

"Yes, sir."

I watch until he leaves. Tia faces me. "What happened?"

"When is Jermaine supposed to pick up Tyson?"

"X, he has rights," her voice tremors.

"Every time Brand X hits the papers that fool pops up." It's like he has alerts on us. "I've said it once, and I'm saying it again. The moment he drags Tyson into his bullshit, his ass is mine." I turn and head to my office. I need to do something with this energy or I'll liable to hurt someone.

"X—"

"I said what I said. I don't play when it comes to mine or my bread. Point. Blank. Period."

"*J*think I picked the wrong dress." I yank the scoop of my neckline, but the material only snaps lower. I groan.

"I forgot you had them." Charlee sips her Coke.

I glance over, confused. "Had what?"

"Titties."

The guys howl, and I throw a fry across the table. "I don't need your jokes tonight Charlee. This is my first date in years." I glance down, and all I can see is cleavage. *Why did I pick this dress?*

Xavier.

He made me do it. It's the most truthful and straightforward answer to my half-naked state. In four days, I've learned, he's a patient man. I assumed he'd call nonstop, but he didn't. But his presence was felt.

Second, I learned the man has impeccable taste in flowers. It started Tuesday morning with the daily deliveries. Every bouquet larger than the last until my office resembled a funeral home. Flowers covered nearly every available surface. I regifted them to the guys because I couldn't concentrate. Every inhale made me think of Xavier.

Now my stomach is tied in a massive knot.

"Between us, I think we have this dating thing down." Harper perks up.

"Speak for yourself. Things with Max are rocky as hell." Parker says. She reunited with her first love, and apparently, it's not going well.

"Let's get to the bottom of this. You obviously like the guy." Hunter sits forward. I'm still surprise we manage to squeeze ten women in a booth. But we do.

"Did you see the length of that dress?" Charlee jokes.

Harper shakes her head but laughs too. "Tell us about him."

"I'd rather not. I don't have time for anything serious. It's one night. Hopefully, a long night, if you get my drift. Then I'm back to business."

"Explain this, please. Why are you going then?" Hunter asks.

"Honestly?" I turn towards her.

"No heifa lie to us." Charlee barks.

"Charlee Raine, you got one more shot." She's a firecracker, but I'm about to throttle her.

"What?! I tired off y'all sitting around complaining and sipping on wine while I'm drinking this flat-ass soda thanks to having a small human latched to my breast twenty-four seven. So, I'm sorry, I have sore nipples, not sympathy or patience."

"Here-here." Harper and Taylor tap their glasses of sweet tea with her flat Coke. Both of them are nursing too.

"Fine! I'm tired of batteries."

Glances pass around the table, and the guys burst into laughter again. The ten of us fill the bar with our gasps for air, and it loosens the tension in my shoulders.

"*Shyte*...that's all you had to say. You're trying to get your back cracked." Charlee slaps a high five with Jordan.

"Why, Lord?" I glance up at the ceiling. "No, I want to have fun, and hopefully it will lead to a little release."

"Well, my advice is to focus on the fun, not the release." Payton nudges me with her shoulder.

"But if it turns into more, you have to tell us about this mystery man and send our gratitude for the flowers," Harper adds, I see the stars in her eyes, and I don't want that—the commitment, the requirement of being held accountable to someone other than myself. Honestly, I want to have a good time and the *D*.

Men can't handle my schedule, my drive. I'd rather be alone.

"That's enough, man talk. Tell us more about how it feels to be a partner at Colin, Baker & Garrett." Alex shifts the conversation. I relax a little and tell my guys about the week because it wasn't what I expected. I'm a partner, but the pressure of being the first seems overwhelming.

"I can't believe you're the first female African American partner. You'd think we'd be done with first like that, by now." Payton sips her wine, and I agree.

"We're not, and I thought…I don't know. That I'd feel relieved and not so pressed. But now my billable hours increase, my rates are higher, and I need to bring in more clients."

"Damn. That sounds like a new form of slavery."

"Nah sis, it's the good old boys club. We gain access, but the playing field is still skewed."

Jordan sits back with a somber look on her face. "That's why I love working on a contract basis. I'd rather work twice as hard then fight to fit in."

I understand. Jordan is the "wild child" of our bunch with her piercings and tattoos. She adds her unique style —a mashup between quirky and weird—and she's a tech badass. Payton and I are the only ones still tied to corporate America. The rest of the guys either have their own businesses or work with their husbands. But we all carry our weight when it comes to Platinum Prestige.

I drain my glass and check the time. "Any parting advice?"

"Be careful." Harper squeezes me in a side hug.

"Text us when you make it home," Hunter says.

"Give the guy a chance," Taylor adds.

"Don't put your drink down." Chase issues a warning glance, and Jordan nods in agreement.

"Yes, ma'am." Chase manages artists and drugging at those events is more common than I realized.

"Call me if you need a ride. I'm heading back to the office." Parker chimes in.

"Forget all of these rules and have fun for a change." Alex winks.

Charlee sits forward, looking straight in my eyes. "And if all else fails, tell him you roll with some real ones. We'll find him and turn his ass into fish food if he hurts you."

I shake my head, refusing to deal with her. But I love her and them.

We met in high school and living life with them is the best. I stand up and shake off my nervous energy. "Give me a hug before I chicken out."

The guys stand. We squeeze into a group hug. I have a few minutes before Xavier arrives and for an odd reason, I don't want the guys to see him. Not when it's not serious because I believe Charlee when she says she'd cut him.

I step back. "How do I look?" I turn in a circle and look over my shoulder. I bought this dress just for tonight. It's short and fitted. I paired it with heels since Xavier is tall. I decide to follow Alex's advice. I'm having fun tonight.

"Let me see you shake it," Charlee calls out.

I wiggle, and they laugh. I wave off strutting my stuff to the tune of their loud catcalls and whistles. I have the best friends in the world.

I'm on my own.

I stroll across S&J snapping my fingers to the live

music. I check my purse before reaching the door. My cellphone has a full charge, I have cash, and my heat is resting securely in my handbag.

I push the door open, and I'm startled. Xavier is leaning back against an SUV outside the door.

"Counselor." He's dressed in all black with Giuseppe's on his feet. I see the contour of his chiseled body through the shirt stretched beneath a black dress jacket. His smile holds a boyish charm, but his eyes are balls of flames. "I think you're looking for trouble tonight."

His list of attributes increases. I'll add that he is the epitome of laid back—his vibe, his presence, his energy.

I stop in front of him. "I hope I didn't keep you waiting long."

"I stepped in, and you were entangled in a group hug." He shrugged. "I thought I'd give you a minute."

"We were having a little celebratory drink. Thank you very much."

"Oh…that's exactly what I thought." He chuckles.

"Hush." I shake my head laughing with him. "So, what do we have planned for this evening?"

"Trying to change the subject?"

"Absolutely."

He laughs, reaching for the door, extending a hand to help me inside. "Are you ready?"

"I hope so," I mumble under my breath. I take his hand and the chemistry between us is stronger than before. I hurry to get inside to break his hold on me, but

I'm frozen, staring in his eyes. "Can I keep it one hundred?"

"Always."

"I don't have time for a relationship." My heart is vying for a slot at the Kentucky Derby. Running fast and hard.

"Okay." The corner of his mouth turns up, and I notice his full lips.

"I'm serious Xavier."

"I got you." He closes the door. He stands outside for a moment before circling the SUV.

Xavier climbs inside, closing the door. The only sound I hear is my heart. I inhale, hoping to get control of my senses, and the scent of his cologne fills my nose.

"People call me X."

"I like Xavier." He turns draping a hand over the steering wheel. I get to examine him up close as lights from oncoming cars, come and go. We're both content with assessing each other. His skin appears baby soft without a blemish. "How old are you?"

"Does it matter?"

"Are you legal?"

"I see we're going to have an entertaining night." He turns over the engine.

"That's not an answer."

"Fasten your seatbelt."

I do. But I'm still waiting. "Twenty four?"

"How old are you?"

My mouth snaps closed.

"I'll tell when you tell." He pulls out into traffic. Then glances over at me. I'm starting to dislike that little sly smile. "How was your first week as a partner?"

"Good, I guess."

"You guess?"

I shrug. Sitting in this fancy box feels intimate and comfortable. It could be the vehicle or the man or both. I look at him as the SUV rolls to a stop.

"Have you ever wanted something for so long that the real thing doesn't compare?"

"No, I can't say that I have."

"Never?"

He shakes his head. "Nah, because the real thing is what you make it."

The SUV rolls forward, and his words turn over in my mind. It's an interesting spin. *This promotion is what I make it.* I store the thought for later review.

We park. I glance outside the window at a building that resembles a night club. I haven't been to a real club since college. It's probably best if I keep that thought to myself since he looks even younger up close.

He comes around to open my door. He helps me out, and now we're standing face to face.

"Just tell me you're legal."

"I'm legal."

"This is funny to you?" That little smile is stuck on his face.

"No. What will it take for you to relax?" He drops his

hands in front of him. The intensity in his eyes is more intimate than sitting alone in the SUV.

"X?" Someone calls from over his shoulder.

"I'll be there." He responds without breaking eye contact.

I glance over his shoulder at the people gathering at the door. "Are they waiting for us?"

"Focus on me. What do you need?"

I think for a second, and the speed dating questions come to mind. "What's your full name?"

"Xavier Evans. And you?" I clam up. "You have to give to get."

"Ryann Gibson." His discreet nod prompts my next question. "What do you do for a living?"

"I'm CEO of Brand X Entertainment. And you?"

"I'm a lawyer. Wait…you're a waiter and a CEO?"

"I wasn't a waiter, I *was* the brand manager. And yes, I held both positions at the same time. Next."

"Why didn't you say something?"

"It's moot at this point."

We stare at each other as I digest this information.

"How old are you?"

"Twenty three. And you?"

"Twenty three?" I step back, and he steps forward. I'm inches from the SUV, and his body is inches from mine.

"Answer the question, Ryann." His sinful eyes set my body ablaze, and he's only twenty-three years old.

"I'll be thirty in a couple of weeks. Are you married?"

"No. When?"

I tell him the date. "Have a girlfriend?"

"No."

"Play both sides of the field?"

"Hell, no." I roll my neck, but the dude doesn't blink. "To each his own, but that's not how I roll. Now, are we ready?"

I look back over his shoulder. There's a woman who looks exactly like him. She's striking. "Your sister?"

Xavier glances back, and his face softens. "My twin."

He's a twin, and Xavier Evans is intense. I glance over his shoulder, and he obviously loves his family.

I have a million more questions. What is Brand X? Why are we here? Why did he ask me out? But I assume they'll all be moot once the night is over because tomorrow it's back to normal.

"I'm ready."

Xavier turns around, and I look up at him. "You didn't ask me if I'm dating someone."

His eyes caress my face before lingering over my mouth. "I didn't have to. Let's go."

A hand rests on my lower back, and he guides me forward. "Ryann, this is my big sister, by less than a minute, Tia."

"Nice to me you." I shake her hand.

"This is my father…" My head snaps in his direction. "I work with my family."

I glance back at the older version of Xavier. This man is not what I expected.

"I apologize." I extend a hand. "Ryann Gibson."

"Malcolm Evans and my wife, Kathryn Evans."

This started out as a casual, hope-to-get-laid date, and now I'm meeting the man's parents. I don't know if I'm ready for any of this.

"X, we need to get moving. The acts are waiting for you." Tia's eyes pass between us before settling on him.

Xavier nods turning in my direction. The question waiting for my response is the same as before, *Are you ready?*

He leans forward, "Breathe ma. I got you." The feel of his breath against my neck sends chills up my spine.

"Mr. Evans lead the way."

CHAPTER 4

"*Y*ou ain't said nothing but a thang!" Xavier takes my hand, leading me inside.

I laugh, and his sexy smile returns as we enter the unmarked building. The dark entryway makes it hard to see. I lean in closer to his body, walking just over his shoulder. The base from the music is pulsing through my body.

Xavier is stopped every few steps.

"What's up X?"

"Yo X."

"What's good with you, X?"

This is a constant chorus as we make our way forward. He speaks to all of them. They part like the Red Sea, letting us pass through without issue. I glance up, and he's in his zone. Clearly. We clear a wide entryway and stop at a guardrail. It's a dead end. The crowd behind us merges back into a massive blob. I glance up at him.

"Where are we?" I yell. But he obviously couldn't hear me because he tilts his ear closer to my mouth. "Where are we?"

"The Dungeon."

Xavier scans the area around us. The floor bottoms out to a large dance floor beneath us. *What in the world?*

"It gets better." He says in my ear, and he kisses the tender space between my ear and my neck.

My moan is swallowed in the sounds of The Dungeon. He pulls me in front of him and cages me between his arms. He holds on to the rail, protecting me from the flow of traffic.

"I have a VIP lounge up there." He tilts his head up. I see a landing above. "We can stay or go."

"Let's stay," I yell, rolling my body to the music.

I turn around to the club safe between the barriers, he calls arms. I take it all in as he talks with Tia. His arms keep the traffic from bumping into me. The original floor plan must have been two stories with a basement. The first floor is ground level, and someone gutted out the middle. Then I notice the stage below us and a band.

I circle in his arms until my chest is against his, tipping forward until my mouth is inches from his ear. His scent is all things male—strong, potent, sexy. "I love live music."

He pulls back glancing into my eyes. "Really? What else do you love?"

"Dancing," I say, but I know he can't hear me. These

are things I love but never have time for, unless I count dancing alone in the mirror.

The music slows to a sensual slow song, and he steps closer. "Dance with me."

My hot pocket is baking, and if this man's mouth brushes against my ear again, I might explode. It's been *that* long. "Is that a question or a command?"

"Which will it take to get a yes?" His breath is a hot caress inches from my mouth.

"Just ask."

"Will you dance with me, Ryann?" His large hands grip my hips, curling around until his fingertips rest on my butt.

"Yes. But where?" I glance over my shoulder to the dance floor beneath us.

"Here baby." He whispers, his lips brushing my ear as he brings my body to his.

The music flows to a hot sultry joint, and I let the music take me away. Xavier wraps my arms around his neck.

Chest to chest. Hips to hips. Heat to heat. Protected in his strong arms.

He rolls catching each move and grind of my hips. I turn in his arms until my ass is against him. I throw it back and feel the thickness of his manhood pressed against me. I glance back, and his heated pools of coffee brown eyes make me moist.

The songs flow from slow too fast. He doesn't miss a

beat, and neither do I. I can't remember the last time I felt free to dance. The beat drops, and it got us moving like he's sexing me with my clothes on. Hands roaming up and down my thighs. Fire racing from his body to mine. Then out of need, I capture his mouth.

Xavier the patient man, the laid-back man, becomes like liquid latex covering my body. I nibble on his lips, hungry for more. His tongue sweeps from side to side.

"Ryann."

I open for him. Our kiss churns my desire. His lips work mine, and I can't get close enough, and he can't get deep enough. His fingertips dig into my skin through the thin fabric, his hardness rubbing me, awakening my need for more, in a room with hundreds of people.

Our heavy panting blends with the thick 808 beat bumping through the club, his body branding mine, his lips sealing any doubts of where I'll be later tonight.

I pull back, powerless to the inevitable. His gaze is mad with lust, and I'm ready to find a private place, to have him all to myself. Because I want Xavier now.

"Counselor." He whispers across my lips before his tongue thrusts inside my mouth again. I suck, letting him know I give as good as I get. His moan passes between us.

"Yes, X."

His smile reflects his pleasure in hearing me call him X. He curls a finger in my direction. I move closer as if that's even humanly possible. "Having you will be an absolute treat."

I'm done.

Done. Done.

"X, it's time." His size is like a massive wall. He rolls back his shoulder, and I see Tia.

"Time for what?" I ask him.

"You'll see."

CHAPTER 5

My stress level is off the chart. I thought leaving my job would lessen the burden, but it was only the beginning while preparing for this listening party slash celebration. Flying from New York to Los Angeles to meet with record labels and the whole Jermaine and Tyson situation.

Had I not invited Ryann tonight I would have passed and missed my own party and missed kissing her. I tighten my grip on her hand as we climb the stairs to the VIP Lounge.

"The Dungeon is our most impressive piece of commercial real estate." I glance back at her.

"I've never seen anything like it."

"I wanted to own a place to scout talent and test new music. So, many of the tracks you hear can't be heard anywhere else. Our DJs mix them in with the current hits to get a gauge on the marketability of a song."

"That's smart. So, this is Brand X?"

"Yes and no." I step back opening the door for her. We enter, and I remove my jacket, hanging it on a hook by the door. She stands near the glass looking out over the club. "You can get comfortable. We'll be alone up here."

She spins around, and the heat in her eyes makes my shit hard as a rock. She's loosening up, and I feel like I'm meeting a different version of Ryann. The short dress, high heels, her hair pulled away from her face, falling into a chic bob. Her skin is a tasty shade of Hersey brown, and I'm down for all of it.

This woman is classy and sexy at the same time. Most would probably say she's out of my league. But in my world, it's about heart and grind. And I got plenty of both.

"Would you like a drink?"

"Cold water would be amazing." She turns back to the view. "So, the building was two stories, and you gutted the first floor to expose the basement."

"Yes. It had to be different. I added this as a VIP lounge. We have a couple of dressing rooms down the hall and an elevator with access to all three levels."

She nods, taking the bottle of water. "Do you rent the space out?"

"We haven't, but we'd consider it. Why? What do you have in mind?" I sit on the couch and pat the space beside me. I reach for the remote.

"Have you heard of Platinum Prestige?" She sits back, turning her body towards me.

"Yes. My boy Marques mentioned it in passing."

"He's actually one of our clients and my favorite R&B singer."

"You represent him?"

"No, I'm a partner. We're an upscale concierge service, anything from chartering a private flight to delivering a box of chocolates."

"Word? You practice law and do that?"

"Yes. They really are one and the same since I handle the legal matters—contracts, negotiations, securing services, and such."

I sit back, surprised. This woman has layers. I open my mouth to ask another question when I hear a knock at the door. I walk over, and it's Tia.

I let her inside. "Ready?"

"Yes. Are the folks are heading up?"

"Yes, they're right behind me." She leans in closer, "I wanted to make sure you two were decent before they come in."

"Good looking out."

Tia laughs and opens the door for our folks. I grab the microphone from her and walk over to the sitting area. I sit on the loveseat near the open window towards the club.

I lean forward, "Will you join me, Ryann?" I smile pleased to have her beside me.

I take the earpiece from Tia. I call down to the DJ booth to ensure he's ready. After getting the green light, I use the remote to open the window. Then I take the mic.

"Are y'all having a good time tonight?" The crowd goes wild. "I like the sound of that. Tonight, is a very special night." I glance over at Ryann. "We're celebrating Brand X with this surprise concert featuring all of our artists. Ready for the first act?"

I wait for the roar to flood the VIP Lounge. "Then give it up for Austin's own, Cash."

CHAPTER 6

I dance and party until I can't stand. X is carrying my shoes, and he offered to carry me, but I feel embarrassed enough about walking around in his socks.

"Babe, the sidewalks are filthy out there. How about I carry you from the door to my ride?"

"X, I don't care if you throw that sly-ass smile my way." I try to raise my voice, but my head is already throbbing. I drink wine, not hard liquor. Tonight, I did both.

"Sly ass?" He's fighting to hold back his laughter.

"And don't laugh at me." I rock a little trying to hold it together. I'm so glad it's Friday. Or is it Saturday morning? I'm going home and sleeping all day.

"How many shots did you have?"

"I can't remember." I stopped counting after five. I was having a good ass time with Malcolm, Kathryn, Tia,

and his staff. Everything was perfect. And the concert...
"X, this was the best date of my life."

"Is it the alcohol talking?" He leans forward and kisses me.

"Maybe, but not really." We laugh.

"How about you ride my back?"

"I can't my dress is too short." I whine.

"Hold that thought." He runs off.

We're back on the main floor. It's four in the morning, and The Dungeon is closed. The staff is cleaning up and restocking. Then X returns with a gym bag. He digs around and pulls out some blue basketball shorts.

"You're just trying to get me out of my dress." I tease.

"Duh."

I playfully smack his chest. "Do you have a shirt too? And they better not be dirty." I smell the shorts.

His hand dives back into the bag. "It's this or I can carry you like a caveman over my shoulder."

"Give it to me." I snatch the shirt, and he pats my butt as I head to the ladies' room.

"We'll leave when you get back."

"Cool." I wave my hand in the air. All I want is a pillow. I enter the bathroom. I use some tissue to whip the toilet, praying I don't catch something, but I have to sit or lay down.

I slip on the shorts and start peeling off the dress when I hear talking in the bathroom. I pay it no mind, I'm almost out of the dress. Now to put on the shirt.

"Who is that with X?"

"Nobody. She'll be here today, gone tomorrow."

The door opens and closes. I toss my dress over my shoulder. I step out, and I'm alone. I dismiss what I heard. I'm not looking for anything serious. I wanted to have a good time I did. I wanted to get laid, I didn't do that, but I'm not letting bathroom chatter ruin my night or day.

I wash my hands and try to press my makeup back in place with a damp paper towel. It's hopeless. I open the bathroom door, and X is waiting for me.

His smile is bright, but he looks the way I feel, exhausted. He stands up and takes the dress from my hand, tossing it in his gym bag.

"You good?"

"I'm great." I walk towards the front. It takes a moment for him to snap into motion.

"What happened Ryann?"

"What are you talking about?" I dig around in my purse for my phone. I bet the guys are worried sick.

"Ryann?" I find it and scan my text messages, ignoring him. "Ryann?"

"Yes, Xavier."

"Xavier?" He snatches my phone. "What happened from the time you went in and out of the bathroom?"

"Nothing." I take my phone back, scanning the area wondering who it was since there are waitresses and bartenders still hanging around. "Did Tia leave?"

"Yes, she wanted to make it home before Tyson woke.

Let's get out of here." He turns his back in my direction, and I climb up. He stands tall, wrapping my legs around his waist.

We're almost at the door, and I hear the voices from the bathroom. They're standing near the door. I can describe them both at once. Petite, curvy, plump lips, oversized asses.

I'm salty. Their petty comments ruined a perfect night. But I don't want to think about X having another woman, especially not Thing 1 and Thing 2.

"See you later X." Thing 1 says.

"Goodnight girls, drive home safely." I respond. I guess I'm petty too when I don't have a right to an opinion because Xavier is not my man. However, he's mine until we end our date.

X stops in the middle of the sidewalk and makes a left.

"The car is that way."

"I'm not putting you down until you talk to me." He stops glancing over his shoulder. I snap my mouth closed. "Fine."

He walks and walks until I rest my head on his shoulder. *This is nice.*

"It's nothing X." I yawn.

"It is, if you close me out. Just minutes before we were on the best date of your life, and now you won't even look at me." He stops looking, left and right. "I'm hungry."

He sniffs and follows his nose, making a right at the end of the block.

"Breakfast tacos. I knew I smelled something." He stops in front of the menu beside the taco truck.

"Potato, egg, and cheese on flour and water." I lay my head back on his shoulder while he orders the food. "You can put me down."

"I'm good." He walks to the end of the block. "That's dope."

"What?" I lift my head and see a wall covered in graffiti. "I agree."

"The building is empty." He walks closer, trying to look inside the windows. "How far did we walk? A few blocks?"

"Give or take. I can see The Dungeon from here."

"Hum." He snaps a picture of the sign in the window then he glances up and down the street. "How far would you say we are from downtown?"

"Two miles, maybe three. What are you thinking about?"

"Nothing. Passing off the time until you tell me the truth." His eyes meet mine in the reflection of the dirty glass windows of the building.

"I heard some bathroom chatter, and I didn't like it."

"About?"

"You and me?"

"What about us?" That one word, us, makes it sound more permanent than it should.

"That's the thing, there is no us."

49

"Then why did you let it get under your skin?"

"I had too many shots." I turn from his probing gaze.

"Oh, so you T-Paining it? Blaming it on the alcohol?"

"Whatever Xavier. The taco man is trying to get your attention."

"He can wait. Ryann, so you know, I didn't get here by rushing and letting other people decide for me. When I find something I want, I'm an extremely patient man."

He turns back to the taco truck. He passes me the bag, and I hold it while he takes me back to his vehicle. We make it back, and he opens the door lowering me to the seat.

"What did they say?"

"That I'd be here today, gone tomorrow."

He takes it in with a sway of his head. He closes the door, and I cradle the warm tacos in my lap. He climbs in behind the driver seat.

"My place is up the street. Let's sleep a few winks and then I'll take you home."

"Fine."

We ride in silence. I send a quick message to the guys, *I'm good. We had a blast. I'll tell you about it tonight. Dinner at my place @ 7 pm. Text your item.* I hit send. *I'll order pizza. (I'll check back later.)* Then I drop my phone back in my purse.

By the time I glance back up we're exiting the highway and heading towards Central Austin. It's been years since I've stopped through this side of town. Then he brings the vehicle to a stop.

"Where are we?"

"Brand X Entertainment." I reach for the door. "Hold tight, I'll get you."

I climb back on his back, and we head inside a building. "You live in a corporate building."

"No. But I have a place here for long nights. It keeps me safe since my place is in the country." We ride up the elevator and pass a conference room. He inserts a key into the door at the end of the hall, tucked in the corner.

"Wow! Nice place." Then my inner voice whispers, *Did he just take me to his booty-call spot?*

CHAPTER 7

I drop my keys on the table and lock the door then I lower Ryann to the floor. "There's fresh slippers down there."

"This is where you entertain?"

I leave her standing at the door. I can't decide if I'm pissed off at the person in the bathroom or Ryann. Both are equally responsible.

"Xavier?"

"Ryann, I'm tired." I face her. "You can stand there and fuss or come this way and rest. We can warm up the tacos in a couple of hours." Her glare burns through me. I turn around and head towards my bed.

I strip naked and find some shorts. I need twenty minutes of sleep then I can think straight. Because if I talk to Ryann right now, I'll never get a second date. I hear the sounds of her sock covered feet stop at my doorway. I pat the bed. I open an eye when I don't hear her move.

"Ryann, please have a little sympathy. I've been awake for over twenty-four hours. Let me sleep for a few minutes."

She drags across the room.

"Put your bag down because I don't want that gun in my bed." I tuck the pillow under my head.

"Fine."

"And stop saying fine." The bed shifts, but I don't feel her body heat. I open my eyes, and she's laying on the edge of the bed as if my arms can't reach her.

"Whatever."

"You know what, I'll make a cup of coffee and take you home." I rub my eyes, rolling over on my back. I can't sleep if she doesn't feel safe or doesn't want to stay.

"No, thank you. I'll call my friends in a couple of hours."

"I picked you up, and I'll drop you off." I swing my legs over the side of the bed and stand.

"Anybody ever tell you you're bossy?"

"Anybody ever tell you you're childish?" I glance back at her. My bed is the best money can buy for a reason. I work hard, and when it's time to crash, I'm out. This bickering is not me. I need some sleep, and I won't get it with her here.

"What?!" She snaps up, running around to stand in front of me. She's teeing up for some shit. "Don't clam up now. Finish what you started."

I glance down over my folded arms. "Start by following your own advice. Finish what *you* started. Why give some gossiping females the privilege of mattering? Instead, you let whoever it was petty enough to engage in bathroom gossip ruin *our* date. It's obvious who I want to spend my time with. I'm the one who sent you flowers all week. I'm the one who invited you as my date to a significant milestone in my business, with my family. It was you." I thrust my finger in her direction. "Not them, whoever it was. I made my choice. And if you can't see it, well, I don't know what else to say, except goodnight."

I walk back to my comfortable-ass bed and lay down. But I can't sleep. My heart is racing. I waited all week to spend time with Ryann. Our date went from perfect to this. It's mad fucked up right now.

"Xavier?"

"Yes, Ryann."

"What did you mean by 'the real thing is what you make it'?"

The bed shifts, I feel her move closer. She smells like a little of her perfume and a little of me from my clothes. Despite the arguing, I like being near her. I think back over our time and recall the conversation on the way to The Dungeon.

"Life is what we make it." I open my eyes, and she's right here. I reach out and touch the side of her face, then I rest my hands on my chest. I search the ceiling for the words beyond my agitation and exhaustion. "We get millions of choices. Each choice opens more choices.

I have the free will to make every moment count. So tonight, you chose to let them upset you, just like I chose to let your response get under my skin. My fault, I apologize. But did you stop and consider that your best date ever was my best date ever too? And that maybe I was fighting to keep the night about you and me?"

Ryann cups the side of my face and kisses me. Not hot and filled with a lustful ache but it's intimate holding the promise every soul aches for...connection. Not a career, not a promotion, not a possession. But love.

She crawls closer, straddling my body. She leans forward until her chest rests on mine and I take a moment to wrap my arms around her. Her ass fits my hands. Her body molds to mine perfectly. It doesn't get better than this.

"I'm sorry X." Her beautiful face hovers over mine. "I made up my mind before I came that I didn't want this."

"You didn't want me?" I tense, remove my hands from her. But she grabs them and places them back without missing a beat.

"Yes, but it wasn't about you. It was anyone. I don't have time in my life for this—staying out all night, clubbing, arguing. This requires energy I don't possess."

"You don't or you won't?" I hold her eyes, ashamed that I'm checking for this chick and she's not willing to even try.

"Xavier, I don't come and go as I please. I have obligations and responsibilities."

"Just like every-fucking-body else. Welcome to the real world."

"Stop Xavier." She sits back on her heels.

"Stop what?"

"The cursing and angry words. I'm telling you my truth, and you're making it about you."

I push to sit up, and Ryann rests her hands on my shoulders.

"We're staying like this. We're talking this out because I plan to finish what we started. But not with this energy between us." Her words are loud and clear.

I feel the smile crossing my face.

"Don't give me that sly ass smile X." She smiles back. "Talk to me."

She's trying, and I'll have to tread lightly because I want to get to know this woman. "Your truth is a facade."

"What?" Her neck snaps back. I got her full attention.

I worked in Torsion for seven years. Most of those years I served people, day in and day out, thousands of people. It taught me one of the best skills in business, the ability to read people. I'm about to shatter her whole situation.

"So, all of the partners at your firm are single?"

"No."

"Childless?"

"No."

"Do they all work tirelessly like you?"

"No, Xavier."

"That tells me it's a personal choice."

"You know how this shit works. We work twice as hard to get half as far." She yells.

"Only if you're playing their game. Playing their game means you play by their rules."

Her eyes dart off, it's the moment of truth. Her arms cross and remain like a block of cement. She's chewing on the inside of her lip and staring out over the city. I wrap my arm around her.

"I play their game because I want to make a difference." Her eyes find mine. "Do I bust my ass? Yes, because we can't be caught slipping. One slip up and it could be another ten years before another minority gets a shot."

I kiss her, running my hands up and down her back. This is the woman I saw in the luncheon.

"I get it. But is this what you want for your life?"

"Everybody can't quit their jobs X."

"I'm not talking about everybody. I'm talking about you. And who said anything about quitting."

"I can't think without sleep."

"Exactly. But someone was set on arguing." I chuckle as she snuggles in my arms. "How about we rid ourselves of any expectations and start with where we are?"

"I don't know. We've technically known each other less than a week, and we're already at each other's throats." Her long legs circle my hips.

"Arguing only means we're passionate. The next step is to refocus that passion. Use it to benefit us instead of hurting us."

"Are you sure you're only twenty-three?"

"You said, you made up your mind to diss me." She pulls back, wagging her head. "What?"

"Nobody said anything about dissing you."

"Whatever." I mimic her voice to get a smile from her.

"Talk, man." She playfully smacks my chest and falls back into my arms.

"Fine." I hold her tighter again. "So, what changed your mind?"

She's silent. The longer I wait, the more I feel anxious to hear her response.

"You." She whispers the single word into the crook of my neck. The warmth of her breath awakes my need to have her, all of her.

"Explain Counselor."

Her shoulders rise and fall. "I guess last night I saw a version of myself that I haven't seen since college. The part of myself lost in office politics, perceptions, and stress. So, to spend the night listening to live music and dancing it was…."

"Perfect." She nods. "What do you do when you're not working?"

"I hang with my guys mostly."

"Your guys? Who are these guys of yours?" I figure they're her friends, but I'd need to hear it from her.

"My guys are Hunter, Harper, Charlee, Parker, Taylor, Chase, Payton, Alex, and Jordan. We're all females with guy names, hence the guys. They're family, my best friends, my business partners."

"Good to know you don't have a crew of guys aiming to keep me away."

"Well, I do have their husbands. We're amassing a formable crew in that department."

"Good to know." I kiss her forehead. "And what are their opinions about your current situation?"

"They support me. I've never have to question that."

"You're a lucky woman."

"I am," she whispers while yawning.

Her body goes heavy, and I know she's out. I gently unwrap her legs then lay back with her across my chest. This is different. For once, I want more with a woman but not anyone but Ryann.

I tuck the covers over us and glance at the clock. It's almost nine. I kiss her lips and close my eyes finally able to get some sleep.

CHAPTER 8

The bed shifts and I open my eyes trapped under Xavier's heavy arm. His head darts back and forth trying to move from the sun shining on his face. I push his solid as a rock arm aside and close the blinds, which calms his stirring.

I stretch and notice my phone on the nightstand, I bet I have a million message from the guys. Will I tell them about Xavier? I'm not sure I'm ready to explain his age or if I want to open it up to the group opinion yet. I shrug it off, I'll take care of it later.

Snippets from our conversation weigh heavy on my mind. He talked about choices, and I'm not foreign to the concept, but I had my sight set on the title and the bigger office. I never gave the lifestyle much thought, that I'd sign on for more hours and more responsibility.

I'm okay with both. *I think*. I glance back at the man keeping the bed warm.

Maybe it's the alcohol still talking. I grip my groggy head in my hands, dragging to the little door across the hall, hoping it's a bathroom. I still can't believe I had shots last night. His folks are wild. I open to see a porcelain sink. *Yay!* I relieve myself and head back to bed.

"That's a good idea." He mumbles. Xavier retraces my steps. I lay in his spot, appreciating the view and warm sheets. He's shirtless with boxers hanging low on his hips. He's a large man all over with tats covering a significant portion of his body. My eyes drop below his waist, and his morning wood makes me glad we made peace.

"Want something?" He points to the doorway.

I bite my lip, wondering if he's on the menu. I've fulfilled my physical needs with toys and my hand for over a year. Men were a complication I couldn't work into my schedule. But with Xavier ready and willing I'd be asinine to pass on the real thing.

"Uh...water."

Xavier leaves, returning with a bottle of water and climbs back in bed, wrapping his arms around me. Then his cold hands wiggle beneath the covers, under his t-shirt.

Xavier starts a gentle massage fully cupping my breasts. For a moment, I wonder if he'll know how to satisfy me, at twenty-three, I was awkward with my long limbs and thicker curves. But those days are long gone.

I reach around slipping my hand inside his boxers to grip his ass while rubbing against his manhood. His fingers pluck at my nipples until the hardness invokes a sweet sensation through my body. Each squeeze makes my heat rise than his hand slips from my breast to between my thighs.

I gasp as his fingers tiptoe around my bud. My kitten is ready and wet for him. His mouth nips my earlobe, breathing as I moan his name. His caressing is driving me insane, and I tell him.

"You can't control this. I got this." I nod, wanting more. "Ma, this is the sex talk."

"Now, X?"

"Yes, baby, now." He's playing, and I'm about to explode. "Are you clean?"

"Yes."

His thick finger fills my body, and I almost scream. "Good girl. Are you on birth control?"

"Uh-huh…"

The second finger joins the first, and the fucker is talking like we're having morning coffee.

"When's the last time—"

"That's not sex talk. That's nosy." I'm riding his hand, and it's better than every high-dollar toy I own.

He laughs and its as sinister as its hot. "Tell me, ma, and you'll get a treat."

"Over a year." I glance back at him. I see steam rising from his eyes, and I fold. "But can you handle it, is the question?"

He withdraws his fingers, and I grip his wrist. I won't

beg, but he's not about to stop before I experience my release.

"I got you. I can handle you, alright."

He removes my shorts and shirt, tossing them aside and in a blink we're naked. The sun peaks around the blinds providing light for our eyes to explore. I reach out and trace the tattoos on his forearms following the designs up to his chest.

I take his nipple in my mouth, sampling the sweet morsel with a twirl of my tongue. His large hands cradle my head as I continue roaming the terrain of his chiseled body. The peaks and valleys continue until his dick is in my hands.

"Ryann…"

"I got you." I take him in my mouth. His head rolls back, and his hands pull my hair. I bask in the thickness filling my mouth, I grip the base to cover the full length of his shaft and his growls of pleasure bounce off the walls.

"Strap me up."

Loving this little game. I lick my lips. "Is that a command or a request?"

"Whatever it takes to be deep inside you." He produces a condom. The gold-wrapped gift is between his fingers, and I take it. "While you think about it…"

He pulls my legs. I'm flat on my back. Then his tongue fills me.

"X…"

My body's under a spell, arching, bucking, riding. My

body's not my own with each thrust I feel release near. My body's his, and I beg for more unashamed.

"I want all of you now."

He glances up from between my moist thighs with a satisfied smile on his sexy ass face. "Yes, ma'am. Strap me up."

The desire in his eyes could insight an orgasm. But I want my release while he's deep inside me. He sits back, and I take the condom. I've never had an experience like this.

I swirl my tongue around the tip of his head. He pulls back my head using my hair, kissing me hard on the mouth.

"Why are you playing with me?" I can tell he likes it and I like it too. The kiss deepens until we're both moaning.

I open the packet and roll it into place. I lean back, not sure of what to expect. He's gentle, he's rough. He's fast, he's slow.

"What do you want baby?" He stalks closer on all fours. The sounds of our breathing fill my ears, and my heart is near failure.

"I want it all."

He parts my legs wide, as his finger feathers up my inner thighs. His finger dips inside as if taking my temperature.

"I think you're ready." He settles his body between my legs, resting his body on mine. "Under one condition." He teases my folds open with the tip of his head. "Not until you agree."

"This is duress." I whine, rolling my hips, trying to make it slip inside.

"You're overruled, Counselor."

"Agree to what X?" This is more than I wanted and everything I need.

His eyes search mine, probing to my very soul. "Agree to be mine."

I try to move from beneath him, but every inch of my body connects to him. Skin too skin, and I shake my head. I can't afford distractions.

"I can't."

"You can."

I look away. "I…I'm enjoying you and this moment. I know me and my life. I can't be the source behind hurting you. Trust me X."

"I know me and my drive. I can make you happy. Let me."

"I'm good, I promise."

"You'll be better with me." His eyes boldly meet mine.

"We can't even have sex without arguing." I laugh, trying to release the tension surrounding us because this moment will change him and me. *But will it be for our good?*

"I know how to refocus your attention." He grips my wrists above my head, and his mouth covers a nipple.

"X, I can't think…"

"Then I'm doing my job." He chuckles latching back on, and I'd agree to walk through hell right now.

"X, what if you're wrong?"

"Then I'll let you go."

In a single thrust, he fills me. The motion rocks us both. I wrap my legs higher, and his flesh digs deeper until I'm grasping for the little piece of heaven within my reach.

All the air leaves my lungs. All the fight leaves my heart. All excuses leave my soul.

"Yes, X."

"Now hold on."

He pulls halfway out and thrusts deeper than before. I scream his name as our sweat-slick bodies join in a timeless dance of passion until my doubts are drowned out by the sound of our mutual completion.

CHAPTER 9

*T*he signature knock on the front door drags me awake. My body is heavy with exhaustion. Ryann wore me out, and I loved every second. I hear it again, and I force myself to my feet.

"I'll be back." I whisper, kissing her bare shoulder.

"I'll be here because I can't move a single muscle." She chuckles and falls back asleep.

I catch a glimpse of myself in the mirror, I can't open the door like this. I shake my head, turning in a tight circle. Where are my shorts?

I spot my gym clothes and throw them on. I smell Ryann's perfume on my shirt as I shuffle to the door and wait for Tyson to do it again. When he doesn't, I kneel at the door and execute the beat using my fist and open handle like I taught him.

Boom, boom, slap, boom slap.

He does it back, but it doesn't sound the same. Wait ...

it's Saturday. Jermaine was supposed to pick him up this morning.

"Who is it?"

"Tyson." He says, and I hear the strain in his voice.

I open the door and drop down to his level. My Little Man wraps my neck so tight I can't breathe. I look up at Tia, *What happened?* Her eyes are puffy too, *No show.*

My heart breaks for Tyson, and I feel helpless. We step inside, and Tia immediately knows I'm not alone.

"I'm sorry X."

"Don't be."

"We can come back." She sits on the couch.

"I got him. You have class. We got this. Right, Little Man?" He nods, and I can feel Tyson's tears. *I'll talk to him.*

She nods brushing away tears, *Thank you.*

"Tell your mom bye, Tyson."

"Bye, Mommy." I pat his back.

"I love you, sweetheart." She kisses his head and then mine.

"Have a nice evening in class. Love you." I wave goodbye to Tia wondering how to have this conversation with Tyson.

We sit on the couch for a while. I wait for his small body to stop shaking from his efforts to hold it all inside.

"Ready to talk?" He shakes his head. "I know it's hard, but I might have the magical ingredient to make it easier."

He sits back, wiping his eyes. "Magic?"

"Yeah."

"Uncle magic or real magic?"

I grip the top of his head in my hand and give it a shake until he laughs. "They're the same. But you have to be willing to try, or the magic might not work."

He looks off, considering my request. Helping Tia raise him has taught me the real art of negotiations. Kids are the toughest audience. Them and the amazing woman in the next room.

"Okay." He drags out.

"Okay, you'll try?"

"Yes, sir." His head bobs up and down.

"Then shake on it. A gentleman always keeps his word." I extend a hand, and he takes it. Now to see if I can't turn this situation around.

"But Daddy didn't keep his word."

"I know, but every man is not a gentleman." I stand with him, perched on my forearm. I sit him on the barstool at the island. His face twists. I know he won't fully understand it at five years old, but it's the same talk my father had with me.

I open the cabinet. I grab a glass and a saucer.

"Talk to me."

Tyson uses his five-year-old words to walk me through the story. I pour him a glass of milk, and I pull out his favorite cookies, the mint Oreos. I stack a tower of cookies on his saucer and take it over to him.

His face lights up. "Told you its magic."

I lean against the counter listening as he eats the icing

and dunks the cookies. I search for the right words to say because I've always had my father around. He's the reason I'm the man I am and the reason I try to fill the role in Tyson's life.

"People, even adults, sometimes struggle to do the right things, Tyson."

"Why?"

"I don't know buddy. It varies. The best thing we can do is love the people who support us and pray for those that hurt us."

"That's what Pop Pop said."

I smile. "That's because Pop Pop is a gentleman."

He nods, and I hope an ounce of who my father is rubs off on Tyson and that Jermaine realizes he's fucking this one up. One day he'll regret not being here for these moments with his son.

"Uncle X."

"Yeah, Little Man." I sit across from him.

"Can I be a gentleman?"

"Certainly, you have the Evans blood running in your veins."

"Blood? Eeewwwww."

I laugh. "I guess I can tell you the parts you can understand." He leans forward. The bounce back on this kid is amazing. "Number one: Always look people in the eye." I demonstrate, and he mimics me. "Number two: Always keep your word. If you say you'll do it, do it."

"Yes, sir."

"Number three: Family first. Your mother is always

number one." I hold up my index finger and take a drink of my now room temperature milk.

"What about girlfriends?"

I choke. "Girlfriends? What do you know about girlfriends?" My voice is higher than usual. This kid is five years old, not sixteen.

"Mom says no girlfriends until I'm grown. But my friends have girlfriends." His eyes are probing, and I can't believe we're having this discussion.

"Well, listen to your mother."

"That's a long time, Uncle X." His brow folds, and I chuckle.

"I agree. But girlfriends are worse than puppies." I see movement and glance over his shoulder to see Ryann sitting on the floor in the doorway of my room.

Puppies? She mouths. I shrug.

He had a dog last summer, and it only lasted a week. My answer should keep him off the girlfriend trail for a while.

"Tyson, I'd like for you to meet someone."

I GRAB my purse and walk over. I texted Parker for a ride home, and I'm prepared to hear my alpha man roar.

My man. The thought unearths more feelings than I care to dissect. I enter the living room, and the little boy sitting on the barstool turns around. I freeze.

Xavier has a child.

My eyes bounce between Xavier and the little boy. I

guess I need to add a question to my list because dealing with baby mammas isn't in my wheelhouse.

"Miss Ryann I'd like to introduce you to my favorite nephew—"

"Your only nephew." His smile is missing several teeth.

"Picky...picky. My bad," Xavier laughs, then starts over. "Miss Ryann, Tyson. Tyson, this is my friend, Miss Ryann."

Tyson jumps down, extending his hand in my direction. "Nice to meet you."

Adorable. "Nice to meet you too."

He runs back and climbs onto the stool. "Would you like some magic cookies?" The cookie he's offering is missing the filling.

"Uhm sure. I have a few minutes." I take the seat beside him. Xavier's eyes are caressing me from across the room. I clear my throat. "What makes them magical?"

Tyson shrugs, "Because Uncle X says so."

"My boy."

Tyson basks in his approval.

We sit and talk. I learn about his school and friends. I haven't eaten an Oreo in years, and I refreshed my dunking skills thanks to Tyson.

"What's on the agenda for tonight?" I glance at my watch. I need to head home to shower and change. I have a stack of contracts waiting for me.

The guys fall silent and Tyson shrugs. I guess I hit a landmine. I seek an answer from Xavier.

"I think pizza and a movie sounds epic. Don't you Tyson?"

"Uh, huh." He nods playing with his napkin. His sad eyes turn my way, and my heart melts. "My Daddy didn't come."

"I'm sorry, Tyson. I know what that feels like."

"You do?"

I nod. "Yes. It will hurt for a little while, but eventually, it will feel better."

"How long is a little while?"

"I guess," I sigh, I haven't thought about my father in years. "I guess it depends on the person. But I think you'll bounce back in no time, especially with these magic cookies and your Uncle X. You have a lot of love surrounding you and love...love makes most things better." I swallow back my personal pain and focus on his curious gaze.

"Your Daddy wasn't a gentleman?"

"Wow, you're a brilliant little guy." He beams, and I'm falling for his toothless grin. "No, he wasn't. My daddy... is a very bad man. But I had amazing grandparents that loved me. And that helped me when I felt sad."

"What about magic cookies?"

"No," I glance over at Xavier, "I didn't have an awesome Uncle X. You're really a special kid, and don't you forget it." I hug him, and he turns back to his magic cookies.

"Tyson, we'll be right back."

. . .

"Talk to your man." I whisper in her ear, kissing the side of her neck. She playfully rolls her eyes as I open the patio door, closing it behind us. She glances back inside at Tyson. "Those cookies will keep him entertained for another fifteen minutes."

Ryann stands with her back stiff, and I know we've taken a few steps backwards. Her story sheds light on the situation, I'll have to tread lightly. I sit in the chair and pat my lap for her to join me.

"My man, huh?" She sits, and I pull her close.

"Yes, Counselor. It's official."

"After one date, youngsta." I nibble on her neck. "Stop before you have to give your girlfriend talk again."

"Damn right. I handled my b-i-z. And I'd rather cut my eyes out and bowl them in acid than discuss girls with Tyson. He's too young." I laugh.

"That sounds gross. I think you did great with him. Do you have these types of conversations often?"

"No, but his sperm donor keeps dropping the ball. I'm staying in my lane with this one but if he bails one more time." I leave it at that. I promised Tia I'd let her handle it and I hate disappointing my sister. "What happened to your father?"

"Ryan Mitchell is in prison."

"Mitchell? Gibson is your mother's name."

"Yes, and my grandparents."

"The ones that raised you." She nods. "Will I have to drag every conversation out of you? Lawyers are supposed to be verbose. They stretch the truth and have a particular skillset when it comes to restating the facts. You know, and stuff like that."

"You don't know many lawyers, do you?"

"I have a few on the team. But only one lawyer I'm trying to kick it with." I hold her face until our lips touch to lend my support. "I won't pressure you."

Ryann stands up walking to the banister. "You must have snatched this land up a few years back."

"I did, and I'm glad I bought the block." I recline and give her space. Her strength is showing through, and this woman just became more complex. She's driven, intelligent, funny as hell, and fiercely independent.

"My father killed my mother, and he'll rot in prison for life as a result."

My heart bottoms out. I wasn't expecting that. I walk over and place my hands on either side of hers. Her head falls back until it rests on my shoulder.

"My grandparents raised me. But they both passed away between college and law school."

"Do you have any siblings?"

"My guys are it. My mother was adopted, and my grandparents didn't have any biological children." She turns around, like last night. There's no music to underscore this moment, just the sound of the city. "No one knows. So, if you could keep it private, I'd appreciate it."

"You can trust me."

This explains a lot. The number one man in her life disappointed her and took her mother's life.

"Uncle X, the phone is ringing."

I reach for it, and it's not mine. Ryann glances at the screen and answers.

"Thanks, Little Man. I'll be inside in a second. Think about what you want on your pizza. Okay?"

"Okay." The door closes, and I turn back to Ryann.

"I'll be right down," she whispers into the phone. "Look, X, I forgot I have a meeting tonight."

"On a Saturday night?"

"Uh, huh. It's usually the only time all the guys can get together between husbands and babies. Look, I'll call you." Her eyes won't meet mine.

"I can take you home."

"Xavier, I'm fine, and this is all new. Give me time to wrap my mind around it, around us. Okay?" Her hand rests on my chest.

I nod but don't like it. I pull her into my arms and kiss the tender spot between her neck and shoulder because it makes her giggle.

"X." She steps back.

"Come back to me tonight."

"I have a mountain of work to finish before Monday."

"Please Ryann." I tug at the hem of the X Brand shirt.

"I'll try." She kisses me and rushes inside, not bothering to look back.

CHAPTER 10

*C*ontracts cover my desk. I drop my head, closing my eyes. Last night The Dungeon had a line wrapped around the block for Brand X's Spring Break concert. In the months since hooking up with Xavier, we've established a new rhythm. We hang at his place on the weekends and see each other as often as we can during the week.

The perks of being Xavier's "girl" means VIP access across the city's nightlife and front seats at most major events. I'm burning the candle at both ends—working sixty-hour weeks at the firm and partying all night. I can't keep up at this pace.

"Ryann."

"What?" I prop up on my elbow to see Scott slipping inside my office.

"Why are you not ready? We have a client in the conference room." There is an edge in his voice.

"A what?" I sit up, and my head spins a little.

"Please tell me you're not hungover." I open my mouth. "Stop, don't say a thing. You need to pull it together Ryann. You have twenty minutes."

He leaves, and I stare at my calendar. It feels like Monday, but it's Thursday. I hadn't planned to go last night, but Xavier begged, and I promised to stop by for a few minutes. One hour turned into two, two hours turned into dancing until three in the morning and making love to him until I had to leave for the office.

I pop a few aspirins in my mouth and open the notes on my computer. I add them to my iPad, thankful this isn't my client. I'll skim them once I get to the room.

Scott and Jeff, another partner at the firm, share the brand and today they're inking a new partnership agreement. I'm merely serving as an extra body in the room, according to Scott when he made the request last week.

I run to the restroom to freshen up and dash to the conference room. I enter the room acknowledging all in attendance. I'm surprised to see the client is a young African American woman. I take the seat next to Scott.

"You didn't tell me she was Black." I whisper.

"I didn't think it was important."

"Are we good?" I turn in my chair, holding his gaze.

He opens the meeting, not answering my question, and I feel the alcohol burning from my blood. *Why am I really here?*

I scan the room, keeping my ear on the opening remarks. The table is long and polished to perfection. The faces of the parties reflect on its surface, and I get a good look at Scott's client.

What kind of business is this woman running? I turn on my iPad, flipping through the files quickly refreshing myself.

According to her file, Aisha Sutton started a natural hair care company in her college dorm room. Her products caught the attention of a few celebrities, thanks to her YouTube channel. Now she's bringing on partners to expand her brand. I stare at her reflection again, she can't be more than twenty-two or twenty-three.

Five men in suits sit across the table. Two are the interested parties, the others are attorneys I've encountered before. I see want's going on here. They needed another suit in the room and some melanin.

The time drags as we comb through the documents line by line. I flag a couple of clauses for further review as Scott and Jeff negotiate the terms of the partnership.

We break and I pull Scott aside pointing out a few issues I have with the buyout agreement, the shotgun clause, and the provision to protect the intellectual property, namely the formulas for her products.

"Scott, I don't feel right about this agreement." My skin prickles with anxiety as I keep my eye on the suits across the room, huddled near the coffee station and pastries.

"How do you know? You barely read the damn thing."

"What?" I cut my eyes from them to Scott.

"Ryann, you have been MIA for months. While you've been partying, we've been working. You can't pop up and want to rewrite the contract." His expression clouds with anger.

"First, control your tone. Second, you asked me to be here. It's not the other way around. Third, you asked for my professional opinion, and I think you're screwing the girl." I cross my arms. His face is beet red. "And you know it."

"This is a standard—"

"Don't give me that 'it's a standard agreement' bullshit. People pay top dollars for your time. She can buy a standard agreement online. And if those leeches have it their way, they'll pull her from her own company."

Scott shakes his head. "Ryann, I know you're making this some sort of Black thing, but it's not. This is business."

"But you're her attorney."

"And she'll be a millionaire before her twenty-first birthday when I'm done with her." He spins on his heels and walks off.

"Scott." I hiss, and every head turns in my direction. I give an awkward smile, and the others dismiss me, but she doesn't. Instead, she stands.

Sista girl is on point, her hair is laid, and her makeup is flawless. To be twenty years old and surrounded by a room of older men, she is holding her own. She walks a few steps, and Scott blocks her. He talks, and she nods not taking her eyes off of me then she sidesteps him, and within seconds we're face to face.

"Aisha Sutton."

"Ryann Gibson."

We shake hands, and my mind runs through this scenario at lightning speed. This is not my client, but she's a client of the firm. As a partner, I have a responsibility to her and this firm.

"I'd like to take you out to lunch Miss Gibson. Are you available today?" Her eyes are sharp and assessing.

"Let me check with—"

"Just you, if that's not a problem."

Meeting with her presents a significant problem. I feel uneasy, and it's not because of the residue from last night swimming through my veins. Scott just involved me in some questionable shit, and I don't appreciate it. Miss Sutton is waving a red flag in front of the biggest bulls in Texas, and apparently, she wants to take me with her.

I hear Xavier's voice in my head warning me about choices. Watching the way he handles his business has changed the way I see every contract, every deal. Before I saw words in black and white, now, I see people. And this young woman doesn't deserve to get screwed.

"Not here. Do you know where Smith & Jameson is?"

"I'll be there at two o'clock."

The next half hour rolls in slow motion. Miss Sutton requests time to review the contract, and the meeting is rescheduled for Monday. I stand to leave the moment the door closes behind her. I have one hour to understand what the hell just happened.

CHAPTER 11

The massive knot in my stomach is my ever-present companion. I get it when I'm nervous, anxious, overwhelmed. Right now, it's my bullshit detector.

I return to my office and access the firm server. I load every file I see for Aisha to my iPad. Next, we need a private space to talk.

"Hey Siri, call Hunter Abbott." The ringing fills my office, and I turn off my monitor.

Hunter's husband, Ben, was the manager at Smith & Jameson years ago. But it established a good rapport between Platinum Prestige and S&J. Basically, I got the hookup.

"Can you reserve the VIP room at S&J?"

"I'm on it. Don't forget, we have a meeting this weekend. You've been MIA and keeping Xavier to yourself." I honestly wasn't expecting us to last this long or that I'd enjoy having him around.

"Yeah, I plan to change that starting with a house party or something, but this new promotion is more than I anticipated."

"Is that a good thing or a bad thing?"

I toss my iPad and files in my shoulder bag.

"A little of both. Hunt, can you text me the confirmation and I'll call you back? I need to get out of here."

"You got it. Love you, Ry."

"Love you back and kiss my babies."

"I'll do you one better, I'll send them over to hang with their *favorite* Auntie Ry this weekend."

"Send them." Her gasp makes me laugh. "I'm serious. I'll babysit on Saturday. You and Ben can get your freak on."

"You ain't said nothing but a word! I'll have them on your doorstep before the rooster crows."

"Rooster?" I sit back curious to hear her explanation.

"It's what happens when you have kids in preschool, every moment is an educational moment."

"Go 'head then Mamma Hunt. I gotta go." I stand and sling my bag over my shoulder.

"Okay. I'll take care of the room and text you. Worst-case scenario I'll call Parker's office."

"Perfect. Thanks."

"Later dude!" Hunter sings.

She hangs up, and I can see her packing their bags

now. *Who am I?* I glance at my phone, and I can't believe I volunteered to watch three kids. Then Tyson crosses my mind.

I text Xavier, *Slumber party at my place on Saturday.*

Word! You and I butt ass naked on your fake bear rug. He adds the emoji with the tongue hanging out.

Stop frontin' on my rug. And NO, bring Tyson. I'm babysitting. All he thinks about is sex and if I had his skills, I would too. I glance around my office, pulling out my keys. The phone rings.

"Hey." It's him. I wonder if I'll ever tire of his smooth voice.

"I'll get Tyson but who are you babysitting? And do they know you can't cook?"

"Youngsta, you better be glad I'm walking through the office."

"I ain't scared of you." He laughs. "I'm a grown-ass man all day, and all night."

"Your mind is always—

"On *that* ass. You're absolutely correct."

"I can't with you." This man keeps me laughing, sexing, dancing, or talking shit. But I love it and Xavier has me thinking about the long term, which isn't so scary anymore.

I turn the corner and Scott's in my face. "Just the person I need to see."

"Scott, I'm on a call." I have no words for him. I thought we were friends, and I want to keep it that way.

"What was that shit back there?" He sounds like he's chastising a child, but I'm not the one.

"Shit? You were the one poppin' off at the mouth. You crossed the line when you brought in my personal business. What I share with you is between you and I."

"I'm disappointed in you."

"This is the last time I'll tell you to keep my man and my business out your mouth."

"You're a gangster now?" He steps in my face, his voice low. "I can't believe you let a fuckin' waiter ruin your career."

Smack!

His head jerks back turning red from where my palm connected with his check.

"You bitch." His blue eyes turn ice cold.

I drop my stuff throwing up my hands, "Imma go Apollo Creed on your ass and fuck this place up. Touch me."

I'm blind with rage, adrenaline rushes through my body. I rock on my feet, waiting for Scott's next move. I've seen that look before.

"What's going on out here?" Ryker stands between us, but my hands remain up, my stance strong. I won't let him put a hand on me without a fight.

All eyes are on me, and my eyes are on Scott. He huffs and puffs but stays behind Ryker.

"I'm out of here." I pick up my bag and head for the elevator.

"You forgot this." Dominique passes my phone. I press

the button watching the men huddle at the end of the hall. "I saw everything."

"Thank you." I turn towards the chime and enter the elevator. "I'll call you."

The doors slide closed, and I slide to the floor. My stomach grips, and I feel like I'm about to be sick. I can't control the shake of my hands as I see the time still running on the screen.

"X?" I swallow hard, and I can't hold back the tears.

"I'm downstairs."

CHAPTER 12

*M*y world runs in slow motion. One second we're laughing, the next I hear him call my woman a bitch. I drove across town on two wheels, my hands ache from the grip I have on the steering wheel. I call out to her, hoping she'll hear I'm still on the line.

My SUV comes to a screeching halt in front of the building. I put on my hazard lights running towards the building. The moment she exits the building, I exhale. I scoop her up. Ryann's legs wrap around my waist as I crush her body into mine.

"You good?" She nods, but I saw the tears in her eyes. "Wait in the truck for me?"

She pulls back, and I dry her face with my thumbs. "I love you, X, but no."

"You love me?" This woman is a rock, and to see her crying is killing me. She nods, and the humor disappears, she's barely holding it together, and I'm about to catch a case. I just need the dude's last name. "I love you too."

"How much X?" She chews on her lip, and I can't believe my luck. I glance at the buildings around us and the people ignoring us. "Come on... I've heard the chicken nugget version, the stars in the sky version, oh and the Transformer version was genius."

"Ry, I'm trying to get upstairs and knock the block off this dude."

"I know, and I won't let you." Her voice cracks, "He's not worth it. So, tell me. How much do you love me X?"

I guess she's heard it over and over again. I walk us back to my ride. I sit her inside, and I climb in behind the wheel. She turns in her seat to face me, and I see my future.

"Marry me?"

A gasp slips. Her eyes search mine down to my soul, and the only thing there is her. I have my family, my business, but nothing compares to Ryann.

"It doesn't have to be today or tomorrow. I just want us to agree that this...you and I...are it."

"How much X?"

My heart is racing for a different reason. I can't imagine what I'd do if I got my hands-on Scott. And the level of my rage shows me how deep I love this woman. I grip the steering wheel, trying to conceive my best analogy. It's been six months, not without issues or arguments or differences but I wouldn't change a single moment. Our first date comes to mind.

"Imagine The Dungeon." I reach for her hand, and I kiss it. "Think about the floor gutted to expose the stage, dance floor, the DJ booth. It exposes the essence of my operation. Before you, the building was here, but it lacked its essence, its soul." I take a deep breath. "So, take the energy from last night, music, laughter, dancing, and replace it with this." I remove the rock from my armrest. "I love you more than that, Ryann."

"That's a lot of ice X." Her eyes glisten.

"It is. But it won't mean anything if you don't say yes."

"Is that a command or a request?" She climbs over, lowering down onto my lap.

"Whatever it takes to spend the rest of my life with you."

"Yes X, I'll marry you."

I slip the ring on her finger, and we seal it with a kiss. Her body against mine, my tongue giving her a sample of what's to come.

There's a knock on the window. "Y'all can't do that here."

"Yeah man, we're getting out of here." I hold Ryann's gaze. "I love you. Now buckle in." She crawls back to her seat. "There's a bag in the glove box for you." I hear the snap and turn over the engine. "Your place or mine?"

"S&J. I have a meeting."

We cover the distance, and she fills me in on the details. I thought I had it all. My parents, sister, nephew, my business. But Ryann shows me there's more in store for our lives. This is truly only the beginning.

"What's your plan?" I ask parking near the curb.

"I don't have one yet. This is all happening so fast."

"She needs investors, right?" She nods. "Then invest in her business. That's the best way to keep the suits from taking her out."

"I can't it's a conflict of interest."

"Not if you're not an employee of the firm."

She stares at me. "You want me to quit my job?"

"I'm not telling you to do anything. I'm introducing another option."

This is the part of her life she keeps to herself, and I let her. Her business, her friends, her career. I've met her guys a few times, but Ryann has a way of keeping the areas of her life separate. But it seems my diligent patience is turning this entire situation around right before my eyes.

"You change the system from the inside out," she reasons.

"I say change it, by changing that shit. Stop waiting for permission." I lean back and wait for her to take my bait. I've seen this coming for months.

"X, what are you up to?"

"Nothing, I'm just waiting for the boss to boss up."

CHAPTER 13

The silent challenge isn't missed. How can I help Aisha? Do I want to leave the firm after finally being promoted to partner? I dig out my phone and see Hunter's text message. I got the room, now I need a plan. I need my guys. I send the text, *SOS. S&J ASAP.*

I reach for the handle and realize he's still buckled in. "Are you coming inside?"

"I can for a little while, I have to pick up Tyson from school today. Tia has a class tonight." He jumps out, and I breathe a sigh of relief as the messages from the guys come in. Xavier opens the door and takes my hand. His presence in my life is unexplainable. I glance down at my engagement ring, and I can't believe it.

"I can't believe you asked me." I whisper as the hostess leads us back to the conference room.

"I knew I wanted to marry you from the time you dirty winded with me on the dance floor."

"See… I'm trying to be sentimental, and you got jokes." He kisses my neck. "That's better."

I pull out my iPad and start working through the files. Xavier remains unmoved yet focused on me.

"What?" The intensity in his eyes give me butterflies.

"I like seeing you like this. Focused and in control."

"X is this more sex talk?" I laugh.

"Maybe." I shake my head. "I can't help it. You're in my blood girl." He leans forward smacking a kiss on my lips.

"Continue." I turn sliding forward with my legs sandwiching his.

"It's like I got the brains, beauty, body, freak, all in one. The shit is dope." He leans forward. "I'm wondering if you'd consider adding another title to the list."

"I'm listening."

"Legal counsel of Brand X Entertainment." I sit back. "We have real estate, entertainment, artist management, and a chain of mechanic shops. You'd head the entire legal department. You could hire a couple of attorneys to help."

"How are you doing this at twenty-three X?"

"I'm a man with a plan and with my queen, ain't no stopping us."

The paradox of this moment doesn't surprise me. I have three degrees, he has a high school diploma. I have a job, he has a business. I'm a lawyer, he's a businessman. I was so focused on his age that I almost missed learning from a profound entrepreneur.

The door opens, and we turn to see Aisha. I stand.

"X? What are you doing here?" She leans in to hug him, and I wait for an explanation.

"Hanging with my lady." Her eyes turn my way and back to him. "This is the client?"

"Yes, you guys know each other?" I ask.

"Yeah, Aisha and I go way back. Tia's going to trip when I tell her I saw you."

"How is she?" Aisha drops her purse in a chair across from us.

"Good, she's almost done with her degree at Huston-Tillotson and Tyson's in preschool now."

"Wow, I can't believe it. This makes me feel better about asking you to lunch." She turns to me.

"Let's sit and take it from the top."

For the next hour, Aisha tells us about starting her company and her struggles to expand due to lack of finances. We review her business structure, and I'm again dumbfounded by Xavier's input. Then I see my reinforcement.

"Aisha, I hope you don't mind, but I've invited my business partners." My guys roll in, and introductions are made. I sit at the head of the table with Xavier beside me.

"Business, real estate, technology, entertainment. You name it, it's represented in this room. Let's see if we can structure something to help your business take it to the next level."

CHAPTER 14

I see Scott the moment he exits out of the building cradling a file box to his chest. I dropped Tyson off with my folks and met with Ryker Colin. I didn't appreciate someone not ensuring Ryann was safe. He apologized and assured me Scott was released from the firm. He promised to reach out to Ryann too.

Now, to handle this bastard. I step out and lean against my ride, assuming I'm parked near Scott's car. He stammers the moment his eyes meet mine.

"Scott."

"Xavier."

I walk in his direction to put the fear of God in this idiot. My father taught me to be a man of my word and to protect what has been entrusted in my care. That now includes Ryann.

I sit on the hood of his car and make my stance clear. "Stay away from her because you don't want a problem with me. I promise you."

"Gladly." He slams the door and drives off into the night.

CHAPTER 15

*T*he conference room is full of laughter and food. My day gets brighter the moment X returns. The room falls silent when he kisses me, and Charlee raises her hand.

I stare at it, and she stares back. Xavier's face is comical as he bounces back and forth, loving the silent argument I'm having with my bestie.

"Ahem." She waves her hand, and I'm the only one not amused, well sort of, Charlee is Charlee, and that is why I love her. But she's liable to say *anything*.

"Counselor." Xavier whispers in my ear, and it adds gas to that flame.

"A-*hem*."

"Yes, Charlee."

"I want to know how this heifa manages to hide a whole entire damn engagement. How Sway, how?"

The noise bottoms out for a hot second, and then it thunders with laughter. There's not a dry eye.

"What, y'all act like I'm the only one curious? Strolling in like some six foot of yumminess."

"Darius," I yell, "come get your wife."

"You should listen to her." Xavier teases obviously loving the attention.

"Oh hush, don't encourage that crazy woman. But you are cute." I pinch his cheeks.

"Cute is for babies, I'm a grown-ass man."

Yeah, he's going to do just fine with this group, and after a long day, I needed this. My guys and my man.

"So, before we leave, I want to tell you guys something." I grab Xavier's hand. "I'm leaving the firm and accepting the position of Legal Counsel at Brand X Entertainment."

There's a collective gasp.

"What happened?" Harper reaches for my hand, and the dam breaks.

I tell the guys about the meeting and the altercation with Scott.

"I'm not surprised." Jordan whispers. She doesn't talk much, never has. But there's not a dishonest or malicious bone in her body.

"What makes you say that?" I ask.

Jordan exchanges glazes with the guys.

"Somebody better say something." I demand.

"Look, honey, I always thought he had an ulterior

motive." Harper squeezes my hand, and their collective nods catch me off guard.

"Why didn't y'all say something?"

"We did, and you laughed it off." Hunter adds.

"Then we went directly to the source." Charlee states without shame.

"And said what?"

"That his ass was grass if he fucked you over." Charlee rolled her neck.

"Or...something along those lines." Chase tries to smooth it over with a glint of humor in her eyes.

"No, it was exactly like that." Charlee gets another chorus of nods.

Xavier's arm drapes over my shoulder, pulling me close. "Your day ones are bona fide."

"Damn right." They say in unison, and I shake my head.

The emotions flowing through me have me at a loss for words. The conversations start to flow again. Xavier orders food, and I'm about ready to head home and go to bed.

"So, Ry where'd you learn your Laila Ali moves?" Alex asks. We're kicked back around the conference table.

"Uh...well..." I've never told them this story. Xavier knows about my parents, but I've always been embarrassed.

"You got this babe." He whispers over my ear, and I look into his eyes, thankful I said yes.

"My grandparents put me in self-defense classes after my father…killed…my mother."

"I'm sorry, I didn't mean to—"

"No, Alex, I wanted to tell you guys. But I never wanted anyone to look at me with pity. Anyway, my grandfather said I should know how to protect myself."

I cup Xavier's face, scrubbing the side of his beard.

"Ahhh, y'all so cute," someone coos.

"Ryann got a man at home…"

"Now, I know it's time to go because Charlee *cannot* sing." Taylor stands tossing her trash on the trays in the middle of the table. And I can't stop laughing because Charlee ignores their protests and keeps singing.

"Y'all heifas ain't no good." She places a finger to her ear like the old Mariah Carey and hits the chorus. "I can't help it that your baaabee daaadeee…"

"Goodnight." Payton declares, reaching for her purse.

Xavier laughs until tears roll down his face and I wish I could explain this situation. But I can't. So, I don't. It's how we roll.

"Y'all keep laughing, because I know if I had some autotune and a good drink…" And her husband Darius is a saint because he handles all of that. But for all her crazy ways, I know she'll swing first and ask questions later.

A knock at the door brings the discussion and singing to a halt. Then the door opens and in steps Ryker Colin, the managing partner from the firm.

"Xavier, ladies. I'm wondering if I could speak with

you, Ryann, for a moment alone." I stand up and turn to X, "You guys know each other too?"

"We do now." Xavier kiss' my cheek.

"What do you mean by now?"

"The man is waiting, baby."

I turn, and it hits me, "You went to see him? X, how could you, this is my job?"

"And you're my woman. I'm not playing with them or you. I said what I said. Now, go talk to the man."

I've never felt more love than I do right now. He was willing to go directly to the source, despite me wanting to handle it myself.

"All alpha and *shyte*."

"Charlee…" They say in unison.

"What?"

I laugh out the door. I might as well give my resignation now because I got a man waiting for me.

CHAPTER 16

I drop the keys on the table, locking the door. It feels good to be home.

"What do you think about meeting with Parker to buy a condo downtown?" Ryann asks.

"That's cool, this place is here. But it would be nice to get a spot together. I'm grabbing some water you want something?"

I hear the rustle of clothes. "Just you."

I freeze taking a step back, and I see her naked in the doorway of the room. She grips her breast, giving it a squeeze and my mouth waters. I free my hands, and the water hits the floor. I take her in my arms, not stopping until we reach the bed. Moments later, I'm deep inside her, where I belong, and I don't stop until she's screaming.

"X."

"Yeah, babe."

"Thank you."

"Oh, I hit it like that." I look over, and her laughter brings me joy.

"Oh yeah baby, you had me crawling up the walls, and smacking that ass, and…" The slap echoes through the room.

"Keep on playing, and I'll do that shit for real."

"Don't threaten me with a good time." I roll over pulling her against me.

"Tell me what's on your mind."

"I look forward to marrying you." She holds up the ring, and the moonlight hits it. The shimmer reflects off the wall across the room.

"But…" This doesn't sound good.

"I'm not in a rush. You're only twenty-three. It can be now or later because I'm not going anywhere."

"We'll know when the time is right. But for the record, I'd marry you today. So, whatever God holds, as long as we're together, I'm good." She glances up into my eyes, "Seeing you in that board room was a total turn-on."

"You said, boss up." She climbs on top of me, straddling my body. This is my favorite position because I can reach every inch of her body. My hands explore her curves until I know she's ready for round two.

I withdraw protection from the nightstand. She covers my wood and lowers slowly until I fill her. She squeezes her walls around my shit until I can't contain the sounds I make.

The sun breaks through the room when we finally

snuggle closer to get some sleep. I feel her love. I joke and shit, but I'd do anything for this woman. *Anything*.

"Ryann."

"Hum."

"I love you." She lifts her head from my chest. The way her smiles melt my insides make me weak.

"I love you too."

"Even for a youngsta?"

She chuckles. "I'd keep you around even if the D wasn't the bomb."

"Oooohhh… Why did you have to go there? And who says 'the bomb' anyway? I laid it down, and I still get lip action. The disrespect is real. I know how to quiet all that chatter."

Our bed shakes with her laughter, and my life is perfect.

"Oooohhh *shyte* sounds like the kid is ready for round three."

"Nah… I'm ready for life."

"Well, show me what you got youngsta'."

"I gotcha ma."

EPILOGUE

*N*either of us held out very long. Aisha gained the finances she needed between the guys and us. Ryker kept his word and released Scott and Jeff for their parts in the bogus contract. The moment I settled into my new role at Brand X, we planned our big day.

Parker and Max let us use their home for the wedding. We exchanged our vows in front of my guys, his family, and our friends overlooking the Austin Hill Country.

Xavier demanded the right to plan the reception, and now I'm blindfolded trusting this man with my life. "Place your hands here."

"Okay." I hear indescribable sounds around me. "X, I'm nervous."

"Don't be baby. I got you."

I bounce my hand up his neck until I feel his beard and I bring his mouth to mine. "Thank you."

His hands are on my hips, and he starts a soft countdown in my ear. "Three, two, one…"

"Surprise!"

The blindfold lifts and I'm at The Dungeon standing in the place from our first date.

"My best date…." I whisper, and I can't control my tears. I didn't want this man, but because of him, my life has changed. Now, we work hard all day, and party all night. I manage my own legal team, and I own equity in Platinum Prestige and Brand X. But what matters most is, I'm married.

"Technically, it's your best *last* date, Mrs. Evans." He kisses me, and I feel the love down to my toes.

He brings the microphone to his mouth. "I'd like to welcome the first artist to the stage, Marques."

"*What?!*" I start jumping up and down. He's my favorite R&B singer.

"Wait a got-damn minute. You can't do that." Xavier cuts his hand through the air.

I laugh, and the concert officially begins. The DJ handles the intermissions, but all of the acts use real music. This reception will go down in history.

Cash later takes the stage dedicating his set to Tia and Xavier is livid. "Tia…"

She looks at me, and I can't control my husband. The final shocker for the night is Ryker Colin.

"Thank you for sending the invitation." He shakes Xavier's hand and kisses my cheek.

"Thank you for joining us." He heads off, and Jordan slides up beside me. "I know this isn't your scene, but are you having fun."

"This place is epic." Her eyes roam around until she notices Ryker.

"Ryker, Jordan. Jordan, Ryker. Oh, Ryker, you can talk with her about that app idea you had." Her nervous laughter is normal, but the snort at the end makes me turn around. She nods yes then no then shrugs. I face Ryker.

"We'll schedule something."

"I'd love to." His eyes are on Jordan. *What in the world is happening here?* "I'll have my assistant call you after your honeymoon. Jordan, I hope to see you again."

He walks off, and I'm ...shocked.

"What was that?!" I point to his retreating back.

"Me being a fucking freak."

"Men like freaks." I throw it back to make her smile.

"Bed freaks...not walking, talking, stuttering freaks." She lets out a grown.

"Don't give up. I didn't want a man and look." I scan the area with an open hand.

"Does he have a cousin?"

We laugh, and I hear, "Mrs. Evans, dance with me."

Xavier pulls me into his arms, and I exhale resting in the safety of his arms. The music is loud, and the turn up is real then his mouth brushes my ear.

"Ever considered the story, we'll tell our kids?" I shake my head. "I think it should start with...it was love at first sight."

"I like that. Are you ready for this?" I glance up into his eyes, I'm more than lucky, I'm blessed. I kiss him slowly. The list of our difference grows daily, but our love is unmatched.

"I am. I love you Ryann."

"Love you too X. Now, let's turn up."

We dance and laugh and drink. I can't wait for my future as Mrs. Xavier Evans.

~

THANK you for reading **ABSOLUTE LOVE**. Ryann and Xavier found their happily ever after. Keep reading and meet Jordan and Ryker in *Devoted Love.*

It's Halloween.

I'm dressed as a fairy princess. Only my guys get the irony as I cover my tats in makeup and hide my dreadlocks underneath a platinum blonde and pink wig to snag Ryker.

I'm Jordan Cole, the tech whisperer and a partner with my best friends in Platinum Prestige. I gladly hide behind the scenes because I don't handle social situations or people well.

I manage to control my inner freak until I'm stuck alone in a room with Ryker Colin, fifteen years my senior, classically handsome, and the managing partner of a prestigious law firm.

Nothing about me belongs in his pristine life. I fumble, stutter, and I might snort when I laugh. So, when Ryker hires me to build a custom app, I realize I want more than the contract, I want him.

Now the question remains, can I cast a spell to make the handsome prince fall madly in love with an oddity like me?

One-click DEVOTED LOVE now!

AUTHOR'S NOTE

I said YES to a holiday romance writing project in 2019.

Ten authors. Ten holidays. Ten steamy romances. And we've all said yes to taking this journey together.

My ten stories are novella length. I think they're great for an evening of reading with your favorite glass of wine or tea. :) And I had the group of guys to make this series happen.

Then struts in Hunter and her squad, her guys. They came to me years ago. I love a good millionaire or billionaire romance like the next woman. But a few of my readers emailed me asking about a female millionaire. I thought why settle for one if I can write ten. **insert evil laugh**

I hope you enjoyed book one with Harper and Liam. Will you join me for the rest of the year as they build Platinum Prestige—one fly millionaire woman and hot guy at a time?

Don't miss a single release. Join my newsletter at **http://www.janesedixon.com/subscribe** to get updates and reader specials FIRST.

In closing, please leave a review. It helps others find my work and it keeps the lights on, if you know what I mean. ;)

I'll "see" you all soon.

Happy Reading,
Ja'Nese Dixon
www.janesedixon.com

P.S. Again, there are more Steamy Sensations Holiday Love stories available now. See them all on my website: http://www.janesedixon.com/steamy-sensations.

LEAVE A REVIEW

Did you enjoy *Absolute Love?*

Please leave a book review **HERE**. Reviews are extremely important and it helps me continue sharing my books with fellow readers.

JOIN MY NEWSLETTER

Be the FIRST to know!

Consider joining my newsletter? http://www.janesedixon.com/subscribe Be the first to know about releases and specials. You can unsubscribe anytime.

BOOK 1

It's Valentine's Day.

I run to my favorite bar determined to figure out how I managed to lose my man and my inheritance in one night. The man is replaceable, but my monthly stipend is not.

I'm Hunter Preston. My friends call me Jo and I'm the only child to a media mogul. I was traveling the world, living my best life, until Daddy dropped a million-dollar bomb, annihilating my boujee world.

Double or nothing.

He gave me thirty days to pitch a million dollar business concept, or I can say goodbye to my trust fund.

So, here I am with my girls, trying to get more than selfie advice, when Ben, the sexy bartender—who either abhors me or he's immune to my flirting—offers to help write the business plan under one condition. He wants $50,000.

$50k to get $1 mil sounds reasonable until I remember how hot he is and how off-limits he is and how he wants nothing to do with a woman like me.

I'm screwed, pass me another drink.

**Get Your Copy on Amazon
or Read in Kindle Unlimited!**

Read an excerpt on www.janesedixon.com.

BOOK 2

It's St. Patrick's Day.

The day is really not important, at least that's what I thought. I dress to impress, ready to secure my first contract as a partner with Platinum Prestige.

Simple, right? No, I wish.

I'm Harper Price. I've joined my best friends in starting an elite concierge service and I'm up. My sole task is to lease an airplane from Liam.

I walk in, he proposes, I walk out.

Apparently, his billionaire have gone to his head and now the sexy, arrogant menace won't leave me alone. His head is hard as a brick. (Take that any way you want.) And he refuses to accept "no" in any language. But I'm done with love.

No more.

Nada.

No mas.

Yet secretly, I'm scribbling my first name with his last name. Then he whispers, "Live a little Harper." And his money green eyes shine like dollars signs as he throws an unexpected curve ball. He'll grant three wishes, when…not if…I say yes.

Does having the most eligible rich bachelor begging to put a ring on it make me lucky? Hell no!

Not when my heart is screaming leap, my head is screaming caution, and my panties are.…

Oh hell, this is a f'in plane crash waiting to happen.

What is a woman to do?

**Get Your Copy on Amazon
or Read in Kindle Unlimited!**

Read an excerpt on www.janesedixon.com.

BOOK 7

Trick or Treat a Prince and a Freak...

I'm sitting in a luncheon and my boss announces that I'm the first female African American partner under the age of thirty in the history of the firm.

I'm Ryann Gibson. I practice corporate law by day and hang with my guys by night, as a partner of Platinum Prestige. My bank account is fat, my house is laid, but my bed is cold and empty.

Dating at this stage of my life mirrors the setup of a bad joke. What do you get when you...fill in the blank? Meet an old guy? Meet a broke guy? Meet a young guy?

When Xavier, our waiter, asks me out I wait for the rest of the joke. Because he has three strikes against him.

He's young, cocky, and he just quit his job. His confidence intrigues me and our instant attraction has me saying yes when I should say no.

Little do I know, I'm signing up for the ride of my life. Nor how this one concession sets my cold bed ablaze and all work, no play becomes all night, all day.

But when the smoke clears, can two people so different find love?

One-click DEVOTED LOVE now!

Millions of adoring fans dream of having one night with him, but only she has access to his heart.

Born with three commas in his bank account and melodies in his veins, Marques Carter is the rising prince of R&B. But not even his family name can guarantees success.

Brione Allen is a smart woman that made a dumb decision: trusting the wrong man. He blackmailed her family and now she's bound by a debt they knew she couldn't pay.

A chance meeting at his concert leads to an encrypted proposal: One week, one hundred thousand dollars, one incriminating secret. But when extortion and family ties expose them to the worst of the limelight, which secrets will they keep…and which will threaten their small light of hope?

**Get Your Copy on Amazon
or Read in Kindle Unlimited!**

CHAPTER 1

The same time every week for three years and the call got no easier. Brione Allen sat on the couch and blew out a deep breath. Dial the number. Ask for Kayla. But the knot in her stomach told the utter truth. Nothing about this was easy for her.

She tapped the numbers by memory, adding it to her favorites was something she couldn't stomach, not after all they'd done to her.

"Hello."

"Good evening Mrs. Bradley is Kayla around?" She stopped asking to speak with her hoping to gain a sense of control in the situation, but they held her captive with a vice grip on her heart.

"Hello to you too Brione." Her dusty voice held an air of censorship. "I'll call for her."

Kayla had a nanny, private school, and just about everything a little girl could want.

"Brione." She cringed at hearing his voice.

"Stewart, I was holding for Kayla."

"She'll have to call you back."

"But today is my—"

"Talk to you later."

The line disconnected and Brione screamed. No one heard her, and no one cared. Alone in her fancy plush prison, she'd gladly trade for their freedom.

She fell back on the couch and stared at the ceiling fan and her cellphone rang. She popped up anticipating the sweet sound of Kayla's voice. But the screen displayed another welcomed caller.

"Eliana Marshall. To what do I owe this honor?" Laughter flowed through the phone, Eliana was the only person she let close. The only person she trusted. The only person who knew the truth.

"Let's see...I'm your best friend. So I need no reason to call other than to hear your wonderful voice." Brione smiled. "Second, I'm flying into town, and I refuse any excuse you make for not seeing me."

Brione gripped the phone to her ear as she toyed with the hem of her blouse. She'd rushed home from work for nothing.

"I apologized a million times. But you plan to milk it dry," she joked pulling her stocking covered feet beneath her body and relaxed.

"I plan to milk it until it turns to powder if that will get your butt out of that condo. I will *not* take no for an answer."

"Milk it dry *and* add in a level of guilt to the recipe."

"You got it." They laughed. "How are you?"

"I've been better." Brione looked around the room, furnished with the finest, reeking of their wealth. "You're heading here for the weekend?"

"No, I'm heading back indefinitely. Bruce and his wife are expecting twins, and they're keeping a close watch on her. We're planning to hang out in Houston until the babies arrive. Her doctor and family are all there. So, it could be a couple of months or longer."

"Yay!" Brione sat up, excited. "It will be nice to have you in town for a while."

"Just know I plan to pop up on your doorstep and drag you to a party or two while I'm there." Brione shook her head knowing they would have a battle ahead.

"How are you enjoying your job?"

Brione listened as Eliana shared her love of working for Bruce Daniels. She bounced around from Atlanta to Houston and back as his assistant.

"I can't believe the luck I've had with getting this job. It is stressful but fun. I'll be assisting Marques for a while too."

"Who is that?" The name sounded familiar, in a fuzzy, vague way.

"What rock do you live under?"

"The law school rock." She snickered. "I don't have time for anything but class and studying. Well, that and my side gig."

"Side gig?"

"Eliana, who is Marques?"

"Oh, yeah. How do you *not* know who he is?" Her amazement was evident by the squeak in her voice. "He's a caramel dipped…tall, muscled…*god* in living color."

Brione lifted a brow at Eliana's description. "All that?"

"Yes, he's the epitome of sexy. Too bad he's my boss." She let out a sigh. "Anyway, he's an R&B singer from Atlanta. I guess you wouldn't know him since he's more underground." She was all business. "He is the flagship artist of Rockstar Entertainment. We're preparing to release an EP then his debut album."

Brione tried to picture this caramel sexy god. Her failed attempt morphed into her last dalliance that turned her life upside down, inside out, and left Brione estranged from her family.

"That sounds like a lot of work." Brione didn't listen to the radio and rarely watched TV. Her sights were set on securing an associate's position with a major law firm. Fun took a backseat.

"It is, which is part of the reason for my call." Eliana said.

"Oh, it wasn't just to hear my wonderful voice?"

"Of course."

"Yeah, yeah, yeah. Spill it, Honey." Brione walked to the kitchen and opened the freezer, pushing around the contents until she found the frozen lasagna.

"Do you still help with events?"

"Yes, what's up?" She peeled back the corner of the lid

and popped the plastic bowl into the microwave. Then she leaned a hip against the counter.

"Bruce's anticipated maternity leave and Marques' EP has opened a lot of doors for me. They've asked me to oversee the launch with hopes of promoting me to A&R."

"Congrats!"

"Thanks, but hold it for now. I still need to get through this project."

"So, basically it's an interview."

"Exactly."

"How can I help?" Brione dropped her head and chuckled at the faint sounds of Eliana's clapping. Eliana could make it happen without her, but Brione wanted to see her friend succeed. "I didn't say yes yet."

"But you will." Eliana blew a kiss through the phone. "I want to host a release party in Houston, and I'd love to bring you in. It pays good, and I'm almost certain I can get you the gig."

"Really? But I've never done a music event."

"Don't worry about that. Your work is impeccable, you're organized, timely, and you work well under extreme pressure. Are you free Saturday?"

"Yes, how about ten?"

"That's perfect. Get together your portfolio and let's meet at the cafe on Saturday. I'll try to get either Bruce or Marques there too. That way I can cross two tasks off my list at once."

"I like the sound of that."

"You would, Miss Planner Chic. I maintain, where you thrive. One day, I'll grow up to be just like you."

Brione shook her head as if Eliana could see her. "No, ma'am. Grow up to be like you, and you'll be just fine."

"The thought of peanut butter and honey back in business is enticing don't you think."

"Houston ain't ready for us," Brione added.

Eliana's robust laughter rang through the phone. "Girl, if only they knew! And for totally selfish reasons, it would be a lifesaver to have your help *and* get to spend time with you without you skipping out on me."

They haven't seen each other in years, for one reason or another. But Brione missed her too. "I got you. When we're done, they're going to beg you to take that position. And I'll be there at 9:45 ready to rock n' roll."

"Awesome. I'll text you if anything changes. I gotta go, we're about to land." Eliana said.

"Be safe." The microwave beeped.

"I will. Love you Peanut Butter." Eliana giggled.

"Love you too Honey." They disconnected, Brione stood staring at the phone for a minute considering their long friendship.

Eliana was her roommate in college, their running nicknames came when all they could afford was Ramen noodles, and peanut butter and jelly, except Eliana, liked hers with honey or syrup.

Music was Eliana's passion like organizing events was Brione's. However, she knew her love of centerpieces and tulle could not lead to her desired destination.

Brione gathered her hot food from the microwave and walked to the dining room, she turned into an office. She stared at the stack of textbooks. She entered law school for two reasons: money and time. The family connections between the Bradleys and her parents guaranteed her seat. But her high GPA landed her a full ride.

She cleared a space for her bowl, tonight she'd study and tomorrow she'd order pizza and work on her portfolio. She lowered into the chair in front of her laptop, placing her food aside. She opened the oversized law book and turned to the cases she needed to read and analyze for class tomorrow.

She leaned over the keyboard and forked a chunk of lasagna, she cradled her hand beneath it to keep the sauce from dripping onto her expensive textbooks. She popped it into her mouth and did a chair dance as the ricotta cheese and Italian sausage made her taste buds happy, momentarily overlooking that it almost burnt her tongue. She pushed the bowl back to let it cool and read the first legal case when her phone rang again. The little face on the screen made her heart race with joy.

"Hello, Sweet Pea." Her voice trembled, she took a deep breath.

"Hi!" Brione could envision her chubby cheeks, full eye lashes, and radiant smile.

"I think this is the best surprise I've had all day." Her giggle warmed Brione's heart. "How was school today?"

Kayla talked about crayons and finger painting. Her

new best friend and a boy pulling her pigtails. All the things Brione had to experience by phone and not in person. And as soon as the call started it ended, sending exaggerated kisses through the phone to the tune of Kayla's sweet laughter with promises of talking with her again on Saturday.

Life wasn't fair. That was too tall of an order.

Brione used the fork to cut into the cooler lasagna. She had stopped crying about it and questioning why long ago, instead she dealt with it, taking blow by blow and somehow managing to bounce back. But tonight she wanted to sit in it. From the sting of the scheduled phone calls to Stewart consistently dangling their freedom like cheese enticing a rat, reminding herself that she had a plan. This ache in her chest was only temporary.

One day she and Kayla would live under the same roof. Holding on to this goal kept her in one piece.

Kayla motivated Brione to work hard and she vowed not to repeat the same mistake twice. Men like the dreamy caramel sex god Eliana drooled over were bad news. Stewart was one of them. He walked into a room and every woman—married, single, it didn't matter— wanted him. She'd thought herself lucky.

Brione snickered at her foolish youth. None of them cared about what she wanted in life. Her goals. Her desires. To the Bradleys, her parents, Stewart, she was their pawn, their minion, their tool. *So they thought.*

She couldn't afford to crack. She ate the rest of her

dinner, deciding to study first then get her portfolio together for her meeting with Eliana.

To get Kayla back, she needed money and landing the job with Eliana to organize Marques' event could be the break she'd prayed for.

CHAPTER 2

*W*alking into Coffee Confessions had a ring of a homecoming for Marques Carter. He had spent many days hanging around waiting on Bruce to finish a shift before they went to the studio. Houston saved him and got his life back on course. Now that he was back, he hoped lightning would strike again for them.

He pulled the baseball cap lower to disguise himself. The release of his first official video last week gave him more than his usual double takes. In Atlanta, he couldn't go anywhere without people recognizing him, here offered a reprieve. But he didn't want to take any chances, welcoming the way people bumped right past him. It added another reason he loved being back in Houston.

Marques arrived early to meet with Bruce. He scanned the room, spotting a few empty tables and made his way to the line. He lifted his head to read the menu when he felt a soft bump behind him. He turned around and had to glance down at a petite woman.

"Excuse me." She held up a hand then reached out to stabilize a mug rocking back and forth on the shelf. "I was trying to miss the stroller and then the display and…" Her voice stalled as she finally looked up at him. Her lips parted in surprise. "Huh, sorry."

He chuckled. "I think I'll live."

She nodded without speaking as their gazes held. Marques let his eyes survey her light brown skin paired with jet black hair. It was curled softly brushing the sides of her face in a chic bob. Her heart-shaped face and doe eyes held curiosity as her full lashes brushed her high cheekbones with each exaggerated blink behind black frames. But when he zeroed in on her full lips coated with a hint of gloss, her tongue darted out and a groan reached his ears. He didn't know if it came from him or her.

"Andrew Carter." Using his legal name seemed appropriate as he extended a hand ready to see if her skin was as soft as it appeared.

"Brione Allen." Her smooth husky tone reminded him of a midnight radio jockey. The type of voice that held intrigue, mystery, and allure.

She accepted his hand and lightning passed from her touch through his body. *Damn*. Her eyes flashed to meet his as his heart rate tripled. He studied her thoughtfully, appreciating the heat lingering in the depths of her brown eyes.

"Welcome to Coffee Confessions, give in to your guilty pleasure. How can I be of service?" The barista behind the counter asked and Marques was at a loss for words. He still held her delicate hand in his thinking Miss Brione Allen was a guilty pleasure he'd gladly give in to. But judging by the penetrating stare she gave him as she snatched her hand away from his, he doubted she was on the menu.

"I'm sorry, I need a moment to review the menu. Brione after you." He extended his hand towards the counter and she stepped forward. She appeared as surprised as he was. The chemistry between them was as real as the nose on his face.

"Huh, sure." She stepped to the counter and tossed her purse on her shoulder like a barrier between them. *No, baby girl, that purse ain't gonna save you.*

She started to order and the sounds of the room faded into oblivion as Marques scanned the length of her body, the curve of her backside, and...

"And for you sir?" The barista wiggled his eyebrows. Heat rose to Marques' face, *caught*. But her hips were too tempting to ignore in pants that left no curve to the imagination.

"Our order is not tog—"

"Make it two of what she's having." He passed his credit card and turned back to Brione.

"That's not necessary."

"You're welcome," he teased, her expression much too severe for him.

Her eyes softened, "Thank you."

Brione stepped to the side and waited as Marques collected his receipt. They stood in heated silence both snagging discreet glances at the other waiting for their coffee. He had no clue what she ordered, thankfully he wasn't allergic to anything.

His senses were ablaze with her nearness. The closest comparison would be the moment he completed a new song. It gave the dueling emotions of exhilaration and exhaustion simultaneously.

"Are you off to work today?" He noticed the button up blouse and dress slacks.

"No, I'm meeting a friend. And you?"

"Business." She scanned his body in a sweeping motion. He wore a baseball cap with jeans and shirt. His goal was to blend in with the good people of Houston. He wished now that he'd given it more thought. Her mouth took on an unpleasant twist. "What you don't approve of my casual attire?"

"Oh no. I think it must be nice."

He searched her eyes and wished he could read her mind. The barista called his name for the order. Marques passed a cup to her and grabbed his own. The place was filling up quickly. He snagged a table and pulled out a chair for her.

"Join me while you wait." She hesitated. "Please." Brione slowly lowered to the chair. The floral scent of her perfume couldn't compete with the aroma of the coffee beans but it was a soft statement of her presence in the busy cafe.

Marques sat across from her finding it hard to contain the odd sensation in the pit of his stomach. He took a drink of the hot coffee to distract himself. The taste of caramel and whipped cream warmed his mouth. "This is delicious. What is it?"

"A custom drink. It's my favorite." She lifted the cup to her mouth and took a sip too. Remnants of her gloss left on the white lid.

"I'll have to get this again." He grabbed his phone and snapped a picture of the sleeve. "So Brione tell me, are you from Houston?"

She sat her cup on the table, pulling closer. Their knees brushed, her eyes widened. "No."

He waited for her to continue, she crossed her hands over the table. "Are you always this talkative?"

Her husky laughter rippled through the air. "No, it takes me a minute to warm up to people."

He nodded. Brione dropped her hands to her lap, "What about you? Are you from here?"

"No, I'm from Georgia."

"You said you're here on business. What type of business are you in?"

"I'm in a family business. I'm taking a little time off before we enter a busy season." It was obvious she didn't recognize him. It made him relax, he didn't feel "on."

"Do you travel often?" She asked.

"Not as often as I'd like."

"So you enjoy traveling?"

He nodded, "I do. It is a love of mine, I acquired it as a child. I traveled a lot with my parents." He took a drink of his coffee. He joined his father on many tours over the years. "The food, architecture, music, museums, I love all of it."

"Where all have you visited?" The warmth of her smile echoed in her voice.

He crossed his arms over his chest and extended his legs. "I visited, at last count, 40 or so of the great states of America. I've hit the tourist spots. Australia, Canada, South Africa, Rome, London, Egypt, I love it there too. Dubai, New Zealand, India, China, Morocco, Italy, Bali. There are more but you put me on the spot."

"Tell me about your favorite place." She leaned over the table and rested her chin in her hand. Her eyes bright and inquisitive.

"Uh…" her smile made it hard to think straight, he searched his mind, "I can't pick just one. My most recent trip was to Bora Bora."

"That place is on my wish list." A smile danced on her lips, heat coursed through his veins. *Get a grip!*

"Put a star by it. It is a place you'll never forget. The warmth of the water. Its vibrant turquoise color. There's something magical and healing about the island."

Her expression stilled and grew serious.

"Add this one to your wish list too." He wanted to see her smile again. "Torres del Paine National Park."

The spark returned. "Where is that?"

Marques leaned forward enjoying the light in her eyes. "It's in Chile. There's more sheep than people but the valleys are the most vibrant green and the sky the bluest blue you'll ever see. There is a small window when the weather is appropriate but it is worth it." He winked and something told him she mentally noted every word.

He wondered what she was thinking as she dropped her head, brushing her hair behind her ears. Her phone buzzed against the table and Brione glanced down at the screen.

"That's my friend." She held up her phone and finished her coffee. "We have to reschedule."

She stood from the table and leaned over to toss the empty cup in the trash.

"Would you like another?"

"No, I have studying to do."

"Studying?" He hoped to prolong her departure.

"I'm a law student." The glimmer in her eyes dulled.

"If I remember correctly there are three of them here."

"You are absolutely correct." She placed her purse on her shoulder and picked up a black portfolio. He missed that earlier.

"Would you like to grab lunch or something?"

"I really need to go." She shook her head and glanced at her phone. "Thank you for the coffee and the conversation." An easy smiled played at the corners of her mouth.

"No, thank you for this wonderful concoction." He held up the cup shaking it.

"You're welcome. Have a nice day." She turned to leave and he reached for her arm.

"Take my number. I'm in town for a couple weeks. I *really* would like to see you again."

"I don't have time. I—"

"Take it...just in case. Pass me your phone and I'll enter it."

She searched his eyes for so long he thought she'd say no again.

"Okay." She hesitantly passed her unlocked phone, holding the top with the tip of her fingers, as if trying to avoid his touch.

He entered his personal cellphone number and placed the phone in her open palm. "I'll talk with you soon."

*B*rione sat to study for finals, she had two weeks left before summer break. But his voice, his smile barraged her. "Study Bri!"

Thoughts of coffee with Andrew had her head in the clouds. The way his head fell back when he laughed. The twinkle in his eyes when he teased her. It was a chasm in time that passed too fast, she wanted more.

Closing her eyes she estimated his height was close to six feet, the outlines of his shoulders strained against the fabric of his shirt. He stood before her with his hands shoved in his pockets and a killer smile wide with perfect white teeth. His classically handsome features made him beautiful for a man.

People passed their table slowing to gawk at him, not once did he look away or acknowledge their presence. She wondered what his hair looked like beneath the cap but figured it really didn't matter. The man could be bald and she was sure she'd find him absolutely breathtaking —star quality.

Brione shook her head trying to rattle the images of him from her memories. But it proved impossible.

She tried reading the case at least ten times with no luck. But his soft encouragement, add this one to your wish list, rendered it impossible. Adding him to her list sound better. *Forget it.*

She opened her laptop and clicked on an internet browser. She typed in, Torres del Paine National Park and pressed enter. The results populated, her inner child didn't know where to start. She squealed stomping her feet beneath the table to release the energy. Pictures, she'd start there.

Brione clicked on "Images." The pictures before her eyes made her lean into the monitor. There were mountains, valleys, glaciers, snow, a winter heaven. What had he done during his visit? Did he hike? Was he alone? Was it as cold as it appeared?

She grabbed her phone and went back to his contact. And she noticed the note, Call me and let's have dinner sometime. She had stared at it for most of her *non-effective* study time.

She could send a text.

Her fingers hovered over the screen. No. She shook her head, and then what? He'd text her back and want to talk on the phone. She put the phone back on the table. Music. That would help.

She stood and turned on the wireless speaker,

stopping by the kitchen for some water. Back at the coffee table, she sat in front of her textbook. She untwisted the top off the plastic bottle and took a cool drink. She scanned her phone for some music, pressed play and turned back to the case.

Brione read through several immigration cases for class. Her doorbell rang and she glanced at the clock. She wasn't expecting anyone, she never had guests except... She stood up and walked to the door and glanced through the peephole. Her heart dropped to her feet. *What is he doing here?*

Stewart leaned into the doorbell. *Ding dong. Ding dong. Ding dong.*

"I know you're there. Open up and stop staring at me through the peephole."

Brione jerked back, placing her back against the door. She cracked her knuckles and exhaled a shaky breath. Her palms sweaty, she looked down at her t-shirt and leggings. Her clothes didn't matter. But she felt more in control in a suit. Less like the young woman that fell for his smile and honey-laced words only to get stung by a wasp.

"You can do this Bri," she whispered running her wet hands down her pants. She clutched one hand in the other to still her shaking limbs. "This is your space. You are in control."

Ding dong. Ding dong. Ding dong.

"I'm not leaving." He stated.

She placed a hand on the handle and unlocked the

bolt. She peeked through the opening created by the chain. "What do you want?"

"I promise this is not the way you want to handle this situation." He leveled his deadly stare.

"I'm studying."

"I guess Kayla will call you next week then. Give you time to study." He stepped back never breaking eye contact with her. She unlatched the chain, stepping back as he strolled in like he owned the place.

Brione closed the door. Stewart was like the boogeyman. People refute its existence until it pops up under your bed.

He sat on the couch and leaned back. "Are you always this rude to your guests?" He stretched his arms across the cushions, obviously comfortable. "Can I get some water, sweet tea, a sandwich? Damn." He laughed at his own joke.

"You didn't drive to Houston for water or a sandwich. So stop with the dramatics. What do you want?"

"What I've always wanted, *you.*"

Stewart Bradley knew how to pop up on her doorstep when she felt confident, when she finally decided to not let him push her around, then he emerged from the shadows to call her bluff.

"Have a seat? I won't bite."

The invisible shackles clanked around her ankles as she sat in the chair closest to the door. "What do you want Stewart?"

"How are you?" His eyes scanned her body. She

wrapped her arms protectively around her waist.

"I'm fine."

"When did you cut your hair and what's up with your clothes?"

"Stewart I'm studying." His mother was always dressed to perfection including a string of white pearls. He wanted a clone of Mrs. Bradley, the thought of her old sweats and short hair irking him brought a smile to her face. "And I like my bob."

"Is this how you're carrying yourself nowadays?"

"Is that why you visited? If so, we can end this conversation here and now." She swallowed hard.

"Don't let law school go to your head. This is still my show."

"Why don't you move on and let us move on too?"

"There is no *us* without me," he growled. "You got into law school because of me. You can't care for Kayla without a job. What about her education? Her tutors? Her nanny? And don't forget about your pops." His glare intimidating. "I will deliver his career in a wastebasket. Is that what you want? Do you want to ruin everyone's lives because of your selfishness?"

The boogeyman live and in living color. Panic was rioting inside her gnawing away at her confidence. Gnawing away at her plans and dousing her hope.

She once trusted this man and thought he loved her. That was the face of love. It was laughable. Her tongue felt thick and her nerves made it hard to form a coherent thought. She was tired of him pushing her around.

Don't let him push you around. Brione couldn't trust that voice, hadn't she invited him into her life in the first place. She dropped her head, stirring uneasily in the chair, hoping to hide the shame from his probing eyes. It was the cost of trusting an untrustworthy person. A person who valued self-ambition and greed over people. *How had I missed it?*

"Are you done playing with me?" His nostrils flared with fury.

She nodded, fear splintered her heart.

"Good." The storm clouds left his eyes. "Mom wants us to set a date."

She squeezed her eyes shut gripping the arms of the chair. "Stewart you don't want to marry me. We have nothing in common—"

"Nothing in common? We have *everything* in common. Let me shoot it to you straight. I want a date or so help me, Brione Allen, I'll bury you and your father's dreams of sitting in the Oval Office. And I'll ensure you never ever see our daughter again." He ground the words out through clenched teeth. "Understand?"

"Yes."

~

Continue Reading...

**Get Your Copy on Amazon
or Read in Kindle Unlimited!**

Ready for Love Series (Sweet Romance)

Caramel Surprise (Book 1)

Love's Hope (Book 2)

Hidden Desire (Book 3)

Ready for Love Boxed Set (Books 1 - 3)

Smith Pact Duo (Contemporary Romance)

Yuki's Luck (Book 1)

Tempting Asher (Book 2)

Smith Surprise (Book 3)

See all of my books on my website:

http://www.janesedixon.com/books.

*Steamy
Sensations*

HOLIDAY LOVE

10 Authors. 10 Holidays. 10 *Steamy Romances*.

Ten romance authors bring you a sexy story to fire up your holiday. Each author has their own series in 2019 with one thing in common - Holidays!

Check out all of the Steamy Sensations books HERE or my website janesedixon.com/steamy-sensations!

ABOUT THE AUTHOR

Ja'Nese Dixon pens tales of romance in several sub-genres. But her favorites are the ones that manage to keep readers sitting on the edge of their seats lying to themselves about reading "just one more chapter".

Ja'Nese is an avid reader and coffee drinker, who also loves to run, cook, and craft. Her ultimate goal as a writer is to give you a little "staycation" with every story. And she aims to make this present story no exception. Sit back, grab a snack and enjoy.

Ja'Nese calls Houston home with her husband, three kiddos and a four-legged diva dog.

Visit her website at www.janesedixon.com if you enjoy romance, suspense and good stories.

Subscribe to Ja'Nese Newsletter "Reader's Staycation" for reader exclusives, regular giveaways and more.

Stay in Touch:
www.janesedixon.com
info@janesedixon.com

facebook.com/AuthorJaNeseDixon

twitter.com/janesedixon

instagram.com/authorjanesedixon

amazon.com/author/janesedixon

bookbub.com/authors/ja-nese-dixon

ABOUT THE PUBLISHER

Purpose Prevails Publishing
2231B Center St. STE 144
Deer Park, TX 77536
www.purposeprevailspublishing.com